The Further Adventures of Enid Blyton's
Naughtiest Girl

The Naughtiest Girl Wants To Win

Anne Digby

D1440223

*Hodder
Children's
Books*

a division of Hodder Headline

Copyright © 2000 The Enid Blyton Company
Enid Blyton's signature is a Registered Trade Mark of
Enid Blyton Ltd.
All rights reserved

First published in Great Britain in 2000
by Hodder Children's Books

10 9 8 7 6 5 4 3 2 1

The right of Anne Digby to be identified as the Author of
the Work has been asserted by her in accordance with
the Copyright, Designs and Patents Act 1988.

For further information on Enid Blyton,
please contact www.blyton.com

All rights reserved. No part of this publication may be reproduced,
stored in a retrieval system, or transmitted, in any form or by any
means without the prior written permission of the publisher, nor be
otherwise circulated in any form of binding or cover other than that
in which it is published and without a similar condition being
imposed on the subsequent purchaser.

All characters in this publication are fictitious and any resemblance
to real persons, living or dead, is purely coincidental.

A Catalogue record for this book is available from
the British Library

ISBN 0 340 74949 0

Typeset by Avon Dataset Ltd, Bidford-on-Avon, Warks
Printed and bound in Great Britain by
Clays Ltd, St Ives plc

Hodder Children's Books
a division of Hodder Headline
338 Euston Road
London NW1 3BH

Contents

1 *The real Kerry Dane*

'Stop a minute, Daddy!' cried Elizabeth Allen, flinging herself in front of the luggage-trolley. 'Please – I need to get something out of my trunk.'

The long summer holidays were over. Elizabeth and her father were at the big London rail terminal where she would catch her train back to boarding school. Mr Allen had business to do in London today, so had driven her up to the station by car.

They'd arrived more than half an hour early but, to Elizabeth's delight, her friends Julian and Joan were already at the station and keeping a lookout for her. She had rushed off to speak to them at once.

Now the three children caught up with Mr Allen as he laboured along with the laden luggage-trolley, looking for Platform 14.

'You'll never guess what Julian and Joan have just told me!' exclaimed Elizabeth, as her father braked. 'Kerry Dane's due at any moment. The real Kerry Dane herself!'

'And who might she be?' asked Mr Allen.

'Oh, *Daddy*!' Elizabeth was already clearing her tuck box and sports things off the top of her school trunk. It was a smart brown trunk with E. ALLEN painted on it in black letters. 'You know – *Zara's Journey!* That wonderful film Mummy took me to in the holidays. Joan's seen it, too. Everybody has!'

'Ah. The one that you and your mother went to see twice? Starring the young girl that nobody's ever heard of?'

'Yes, Kerry Dane! She was an ordinary London schoolgirl until the film people found her, but now *everybody's* heard of her. Everybody except you, Daddy! And she's really marvellous.' Elizabeth dropped to her knees beside the trolley and managed to get her trunk open. She flung back the lid. 'I really admire her. She's exactly the sort of person that I would like to be.'

Elizabeth was hunting feverishly through her trunk, scattering its contents as she went. Books, garments and photo frames were starting to spill out. But she couldn't find what she was looking for. Where was it? Oh, surely she hadn't forgotten to bring it this term . . .?

'You say she's due here? At the station?' asked Mr Allen, in surprise. 'Well, even if she is, Elizabeth, this is hardly the time or the place to start unpacking your trunk!'

'Not the station, sir,' explained Julian, his green eyes glinting with amusement at the sight of Elizabeth down on her knees, passers-by having to step round her. 'The big cinema next door. The film's playing to packed houses and we gather she'll be stopping by at ten o'clock to chat to all the fans in the queue.'

'She'll get wet then,' observed Mr Allen. 'It's raining.'

'There's a notice outside the cinema,' Joan

rushed on. 'Julian spotted it coming in!' In her own quiet way, Joan was as excited as Elizabeth. 'We're hoping we'll have time to get her autograph.'

'Hooray!' cried Elizabeth, waving something in triumph. 'My autograph book. I was *sure* I'd packed it. It was right at the bottom. Isn't that typical? Sorry, Daddy.'

While the others quickly stuffed everything back into the trunk and closed the lid, Elizabeth stroked the white leather binding of her prized autograph book. She peeped inside. Some of the Leavers had written messages in it at the end of last term. And there were two very special entries from William and Rita, who had been the head-boy and head-girl. What a fine thing it would be to get Kerry Dane's autograph as well! It would be another treasured signature to add to her collection.

'We won't be long, Daddy,' she said quickly, as she helped her father stack the rest of her belongings back on the trolley.

'Now, just a minute,' her father protested. 'I

can't have you missing the train, you know. I'm not sure I can allow—'

'Oh, *please*, Daddy!' she begged. 'I'll never, ever get a chance like this again. We won't miss the train, I promise. We've got half an hour!' She turned and appealed to her friends for support. 'We wouldn't dream of missing the train, would we?'

'Certainly not,' agreed Joan.

'I absolutely couldn't *bear* to miss it!' vowed Elizabeth.

It was the simple truth. She had been looking forward for days to the train journey back to Whyteleafe School. There would be lots of people she knew on board and some new pupils as well. It was always very exciting. And she was going up a form. She was going into the second form! There would be an election for a new head-boy and head-girl as soon as they got back to school and second formers were allowed to vote in it!

'I'll make sure we're all back in good time. Platform 14, isn't it, sir?' said Julian, sounding his most grown-up. 'The cinema's just through the archway over there. Bang next door to the station!'

'And Joan's a monitor, so she'll make sure, too,' pleaded Elizabeth. She noticed that the other two had sensibly retained their raincoats when getting their luggage put on the train. 'I'll even wear my mac if you like, Daddy, so my school uniform doesn't get wet.'

'Very well,' relented her father. He knew how much Elizabeth hated wearing her old mac. He fished it out of a carrier bag and handed it to her. 'I'll get your luggage put on the train and meet you by the ticket barrier in fifteen minutes, then.'

'Oh, thank you, Daddy!'

The three friends raced out of the station and over to the cinema. Although it was early in the day, queues had already formed. The cinema illuminations shone down on the rainy pavements. ZARA'S JOURNEY, they signalled brightly, STARRING KERRY DANE. And there was the notice that Julian had spotted earlier:

Announcement

We are pleased to announce a surprise visit from Miss Kerry Dane. She will be here to speak to the queues and sign autographs between 10.0 a.m. – 10.15 a.m. today.

The notice stood at the cinema's main entrance in front of the big glass doors. A policeman and a commissionaire in a bright red uniform were keeping the entrance clear.

'If you wish to see Miss Dane, please take your places in the cinema queue. Otherwise, pass along,' the doorman was saying. 'Miss Dane's car will be arriving at any moment.'

Excitedly, Elizabeth linked arms with her two friends. Her autograph book was safely stowed in her raincoat pocket.

'You didn't imagine it, then, Julian!' she said. 'Isn't it sporting of her to want to come and speak to the queues on a horrid wet morning like this?'

'She pops up at cinemas a lot,' ventured Joan.

'I've read about it in the papers. She says she really likes to meet her fans.'

'It's all good publicity, I suppose,' grinned Julian. 'It's clever not to announce it in advance, so she doesn't have to cope with a big crowd each time. I can't wait to see my cousin Patrick's face when I pull out Kerry Dane's autograph. 'I shall sell it to him for a tidy sum. He's been raving about her film all holidays!'

'Where should we stand and wait?' said Joan, anxiously. 'We're not allowed to hang around outside. We'll get moved on.'

'In the queue, of course!' replied Julian. 'We'll pretend we're waiting to go into the film like everybody else.'

The shortest queue was the one for the most expensive seats. It was sheltered from the rain by an awning. With Julian whistling nonchalantly, the three friends tagged on the back of it.

'I feel a bit guilty!' whispered Joan.

'It's only for a few moments,' Elizabeth pointed out. 'It must be nearly ten o'clock now.'

'As a matter of fact,' said Julian, glancing at his watch and then at the road, 'it's five past! And no sign of her car yet. If she's only staying till quarter past, she'd better buck up!'

But Elizabeth wasn't listening.

'Look, Joan!' she was exclaiming. 'Do you remember this bit?'

The two girls had turned to gaze at the slim showcase fixed to the wall behind them. It contained, behind glass, a selection of film stills that portrayed dramatic moments from the story. The clip that Elizabeth was pointing to showed Kerry Dane, her golden hair matted and her face streaked with tears, stumbling down a mountainside with a small child in her arms.

'Yes!' agreed Joan, gazing at the still. 'My heart was in my mouth. I was convinced that little Stefan was going to die. After everything that Zara had done to get the younger children out of the war zone, to get them to safety. And they were so nearly home . . .'

Deeply engrossed, the two friends started to

discuss the film. Together, they relived the story
of how the brave refugee girl, Zara, played by
Kerry Dane, had led a group of village children
out of a war zone, narrowly escaping land
mines and enemy fire. Then had come a terrible
journey over the mountains, through storms
and blizzards, with little food and no warm
clothes, trying to reach the safety of her uncle's
farm, in the next valley. Zara had given all her
rations to the younger children and towards
the end only kept herself alive by eating snow.
And then Stefan, the smallest of the children,
had fallen desperately ill . . .

'I liked the bit when Zara made a raft and
rowed the children across the river, one by one,'
sighed Elizabeth. 'You remember – when they
found that the bridge had been blown up? Oh,
wasn't she brave? A born leader. I'm sure Kerry
Dane must be a brilliant person, in real life. It
all seemed so *true* . . .'

'But where's she got to today?' came Julian's
voice, sounding cross.

'Oh!' Elizabeth spun round to face Julian.

He had been watching out for the car all this time. 'Is it getting late then?'

'It's nearly quarter-past.' He shrugged. 'I'm afraid our train goes in fifteen minutes.'

'Then we must get back to the station,' said Joan, looking crestfallen.

'Surely we can wait another five minutes—?' protested Elizabeth.

And suddenly a cheer went up. A car had arrived, its brakes squealing loudly, its tyres spraying water.

A radiant figure jumped out of the back of the small blue car. The mane of golden hair was unmistakable. So were the huge brown eyes and sweetly smiling mouth.

'It's her!' everyone cried.

'It's Kerry Dane!'

It was a thrilling moment for Elizabeth and Joan. The real-life Kerry Dane – at last. And she looked as pretty off the screen as on it!

But then came a disappointment. She ran through the rain, straight past the queues and up the cinema steps. The doorman was standing at the ready, waiting to open one of the big glass doors.

Pressing forward, Elizabeth could see the cinema manager and his staff inside. They were lined up in the foyer, waiting to present a bouquet of flowers.

The urgent hand signal that the car driver gave to the young actress, as she turned to face the waiting crowd, told Elizabeth the worst. Kerry wasn't staying! The car was already moving off at speed, round to the back of the cinema, preparing for her to leave from a rear exit.

From the top step, the teenage actress gave a short address. It was charming and very spontaneous:

'It's wonderful to see you all here. I hope you will enjoy watching *Zara's Journey* every bit as much as I enjoyed acting in it. If you like the film, do please remember to tell all your friends about it! I so badly wanted to meet some of you this morning and stay and chat. But what can I say . . . ?

'Well, I know one thing I can say! It's a lot easier coming over mountains and through blizzards and storms than it ever is trying to get through the London traffic!'

There was appreciative laughter from the crowd.

'So now I'm in big trouble!' she told them. 'I'm due somewhere else later, way outside of London. My driver, who is also my father, says I shouldn't be here at all – but I couldn't bear to let you down. Now all I can do is say bless you all. And run inside and give my thanks to the manager and his staff. Then on my way!'

It was such a friendly little speech that everyone swallowed their disappointment and applauded. Smiling and waving goodbye, Kerry Dane was ushered into the foyer. Most people pushed forward to witness her shaking hands with the cinema staff. What a beautiful bouquet!

But not Elizabeth. Elizabeth was hanging back. She had taken her autograph book out, gripped with a sudden excitement.

'Let's race round to the back of the cinema!' she whispered. 'She's going to leave by the back way, it's obvious!'

Joan looked worried.

'Don't be silly, Elizabeth!' Julian smiled. 'We've only got ten minutes!'

'That's long enough! She'll be out in a minute! I want to get her autograph, even if you two don't!' she exclaimed hot-headedly. 'I'm not going to give up now!'

Elizabeth shot away. She rushed round the side of the building, following the route that the blue car had taken. The rain was getting heavier. She was splashing through puddles but she didn't care.

Kerry Dane seems nice, she thought, eagerly. *I'm sure she won't mind! I just hope I'm in time. You can tell she's in a tearing hurry!*

It had hardly been the moment to stop and have a debate with Julian!

She could hear his voice somewhere behind her and the sound of running footsteps. He and Joan were chasing after her, trying to fetch her back! But for once, the Naughtiest Girl decided, she didn't care if she *was* living up to her nickname. She was not going to allow herself to be thwarted – she must get that autograph!

She had been running fast and was now somewhere at the back of the big cinema building. Blindly, she rushed into the first turning she came to, but it led to a dead end. She merely found herself staring at a fence and a row of black wheelie bins.

'Drat, it must be the next turning!' she realised, as she heard Julian and Joan go racing past, still calling her name.

Then, to her dismay, there came the sound of an engine starting up. She turned.

A blue car nosed into view across the top of her turning, coming from the next one along.

She's leaving. I've missed her! thought Elizabeth.

But, with a squeal of brakes, the car suddenly stopped.

Elizabeth stared, open-mouthed. Kerry Dane was leaping out of the back, still holding her big bouquet of flowers. She was running into the little cul-de-sac. She was heading straight for Elizabeth!

How could this be? For a moment Elizabeth wondered if her friends had somehow explained . . .

No! She was racing straight past Elizabeth without so much as a glance. Golden hair flying, she reached the nearest wheelie bin and flung back the lid.

The car horn was honking.

'Shut up, Daddy!' she cried out. 'I won't be a sec. I can't take these stupid things with me. I've got to get rid of them!'

Julian and Joan reappeared, just in time to see Kerry Dane drop the bouquet in the dustbin and slam down the lid!

Elizabeth was stunned but nevertheless as the actress turned and came racing back, she rushed to meet her, her autograph book outstretched.

'Please Miss Dane, will you sign this for me?' she gasped.

The girl turned on her in contempt. The transformation from her screen persona was now complete. Gone were the pretty smile and warm manner. The eyes glittered, the expression was hard.

'Of course I won't, you little pest!' She brushed Elizabeth's book away. 'Can't you see I'm in a hurry?'

The autograph book went flying out of Elizabeth's hand and landed in a puddle.

'My book!' cried Elizabeth furiously, as she dived to rescue it. 'You've made it all wet and messy!'

'Just like you, then!' Kerry Dane called back over her shoulder, as she ran the last few steps to the waiting car.

She scrambled on board and the car zoomed away.

Elizabeth stood there for a moment or two, clutching her book, speechless at the girl's rudeness.

'How mean!' said Joan, taking the book and gently wiping it with a tissue.

'Did you see what she did with those beautiful flowers?' asked Elizabeth, finding her voice. 'Lovely fresh flowers too – wasn't that a cruel thing to do?'

'We thought she would be such a nice person,' said Joan, every bit as shocked as Elizabeth. 'But she isn't. She isn't nice at all.'

'She's absolutely horrible!' stated Elizabeth.

Julian had not been under the spell of Kerry Dane's film, having never seen it.

'You told your father we were going to meet the real Kerry Dane,' he pointed out. He gave a wry smile. 'And now we have.'

'Daddy!' realised Elizabeth, in horror. 'The train! Now we're going to miss the train!'

'No, we're not,' said Julian, glancing at his watch. 'Not if we run!'

'I'll give Daddy the flowers to take back for Mummy!' exclaimed Elizabeth, darting back to the dustbin. 'That will cheer him up!'

Five minutes later Elizabeth had cheered up considerably herself. She had said goodbye to her father and now they were safely aboard the train.

'You see, Julian! I told you we had plenty of time!'

It had been an embarrassing episode. It had been humiliating. Kerry Dane had turned out to be a completely different person in real life. A hateful person! But Elizabeth had no intention of talking about it to anybody. She could forget all about her now.

She was going back to Whyteleafe, the best school in the world.

The train moved off, then immediately juddered to a halt. Somewhere, right at the back, a late arrival climbed aboard the First Class section laden down with luggage.

Then came the sound of banging doors and another blast from the guard's whistle . . . and at last they were on their way.

2   *Belinda surprises Elizabeth*

'I've already decided who I'm going to vote for!' announced Elizabeth some time later, as the train rattled merrily along.

The rain had stopped and the sun was trying to come out. Her raincoat was stowed on the luggage rack and her damp curls were almost dry again in the warm railway carriage. Her father had been too surprised by those lovely fresh flowers to be cross with her. Elizabeth felt at peace with the world again.

Some of her classmates were on the train. They had caught up with their holiday news and then discussed going into the second form. Mr Leslie would be their new form teacher. Julian was pleased about that. Mr Leslie was the science master and a great favourite with the boys. But the girls liked him, too.

'He's quite strict about school work, though,' Joan had told the others. Being older than Elizabeth, Joan was already in the next class and was now a second form monitor. 'He expects quite a lot from us and is always saying that we're not first formers any more!'

'And neither are we!' Elizabeth had said proudly.

And her thoughts had turned to the forthcoming election for a new head-boy and girl. As second formers they were allowed to vote, unlike the first formers and the babies in the junior class!

'I've been thinking about it all holidays,' she said excitedly. 'You know, the election for the new heads.'

'I can't imagine anyone but William and Rita running the School Meetings,' confessed Jenny. 'They were both so marvellous, weren't they? They were always so fair and came to the right decisions. And we could all look up to them!'

'Yes, the new ones will have to be people the whole school can look up to!' agreed Martin.

'So who *are* you going to vote for, Elizabeth?' asked Belinda.

'For head-boy, I think Thomas,' she replied firmly.

Everybody at once murmured agreement.

'Yes, he'd be excellent,' nodded Julian. 'He's got real leadership qualities. And who's your head-girl then, Elizabeth?'

Elizabeth hesitated. She didn't want to rush what she was going to say. It was important to her.

'I've thought about it a lot,' she said. 'At first I couldn't think of *anyone* who'd be able to step into Rita's shoes! And then gradually it dawned on me – Emma!'

Elizabeth's suggestion created an instant buzz of interest.

'Emma?' said Belinda.

'Isn't she a bit quiet?' mused Jenny.

But Joan was nodding her head. She had gone into the next carriage earlier, to talk to her friend Susan. And she'd noticed Emma sitting with some new junior pupils who'd looked rather scared and homesick. Joan had admired the way that the senior girl was finding time to chat to them and was getting them to smile.

'I think I agree with you, Elizabeth,' she said eagerly. 'I do believe Emma would be just right. In her own special way, that is.'

'Yes. Excellent,' said Julian, after thinking about it.

But Martin looked doubtful.

'She seems sort of shy to me,' he said. 'Especially as she'd have to speak up in front of the whole school all the time. And make sure to hold everyone's attention! Emma's nice but she's sort of soft-spoken . . .'

'Strong underneath, though!' decided Julian. 'There's no softness there, if you ask me. I think Emma's got authority but it's the best sort. It's quiet authority . . .'

'Rita wasn't exactly loud, Martin!' Elizabeth pointed out, rather impatiently. 'I bet Rita was very like Emma before she was elected head-girl. Was she, Belinda? You must have been at Whyteleafe then.'

Belinda had been at Whyteleafe longer than the others. She had joined in the junior class. She frowned now, deep in thought.

'Why, Elizabeth, I do believe you're right! I remember overhearing some of the teachers say that Rita was a bit too young and as quiet as a mouse and might not be able to keep order! But they were proved wrong. Rita was nervous at the first Meeting or two. But after that she was such a success she stayed on as head-girl for two years running.'

'There, Martin!' said Elizabeth.

'Lucky the teachers don't have any say in it then, isn't it?' laughed Julian. 'I think all schools should be run by the pupils, the way ours is.'

'What about Nora?' asked Jenny, suddenly. 'She wouldn't be nervous of going on the platform.'

'She'd be good in some ways,' said Belinda, her mind now made up, 'but I don't think she'd be as good as Emma . . .'

They discussed it further. By the end,

Elizabeth felt well satisfied. Everyone seemed to agree that Thomas was the right choice for head-boy. And apart from Martin, who didn't know who he wanted, and Jenny, who still favoured Nora, everyone seemed to agree with her about Emma.

Because of the way that Whyteleafe School was run, in Elizabeth's opinion it was extremely important to get the right head-boy and head-girl. And she'd set her heart on Thomas and Emma. She felt that this discussion was a promising start.

Then suddenly, near the end of the train journey, Belinda raised something which made Elizabeth's scalp prickle with excitement.

'We haven't even talked about our *own* election! For a monitor to replace Susan. Now she's going up into the third form, we'll need someone new. We've got Joan, of course, but the second form always has two.'

She was looking straight at Elizabeth!

'We all think you should be the other monitor, Elizabeth,' explained Jenny. 'We talked amongst ourselves at the end of last term and everyone agreed. Would you be willing to stand?'

'I – I—'

Elizabeth was quite lost for words. Speechless with pleasure! She had already been a monitor once and William and Rita had promised that her chance to be a monitor would surely come again. But she'd never expected it to come so soon!

'You see, Elizabeth,' Joan said gently, having been in on the secret, 'everyone thinks it was very fine the way you stood down in favour of Susan last term. And that it's only fair you should take her place now she's going up.'

'Not to mention all the things you've done for the school. Even if we *do* always think of you as the Naughtiest Girl!' laughed Kathleen. 'We were really proud of you last term, Elizabeth. We were proud that you were in our form!'

'So *would* you be willing to stand?' repeated Jenny.

'Oh, yes, please!' exclaimed Elizabeth, glancing across at Joan in delight. Their classmates wanted her to be a monitor again, with her best friend Joan! The two of them would be second form monitors together. 'There's nothing I'd like better!' she added.

What a wonderful surprise. What a marvellous term this was going to be!

They all piled off at the station and watched their luggage being loaded on to the school coach. Julian gave Elizabeth's back a pat. There was an amused gleam in his eyes.

'Well, well. It looks as thought the Naughtiest Girl is going to be made a monitor again. At the first Meeting. When will that be? This Saturday? Can she last that long without misbehaving?'

'Of course I can, Julian,' replied Elizabeth, refusing to be amused. 'I'm going to jolly well make certain of that!'

That, at least, was her intention.

3   A grand entrance

On the coach they joined all the other boys and girls who'd been on the train. There were plenty of new first formers and junior class pupils. They were losing their shyness now and chattering away, excited to think that they'd be seeing their new school very soon. Mr Johns and Miss Thomas, who had both accompanied the train from London, checked names off on a list. Elizabeth and Joan looked round eagerly, wondering if there were any new pupils for their own class.

'Good. All aboard. Off we go!' said Mr Johns.

Soon the coach had left the town far behind and was labouring up the steep hill towards the school. A white station taxi overtook them on the hill. There were two large suitcases on its roof rack. Julian, always alert, watched it turn in through the gates of Whyteleafe School, ahead of them.

'I wonder who's in that taxi from the station?' he said to Elizabeth. 'There would have been room for them on the coach.'

'Perhaps it's a new teacher,' responded Elizabeth absently. She hadn't even noticed the taxi overtake them.

She was thinking instead about the coming Saturday. She was imagining the scene at the first School Meeting of the year. The results of the election for head-boy and head-girl would be announced. Thomas and Emma would take their rightful places at the special table on the platform. As a monitor, Joan would be seated on the platform already. Then any new monitors required would be chosen by their respective classmates. Elizabeth would proudly leave the second form benches and take her place up on the platform with Joan and the rest.

Together with the other monitors they would

be helping their fine new head-girl and head-boy to govern the school . . .

The coach pulled up.

'We're here now, everyone.'

That was Emma's voice. The senior girl was standing at the exit, helping the teachers. Some of the new pupils were clambering about, peering out of the windows, trying to get a good look at their new school.

'No kneeling on seats, please,' she said, quietly but firmly. 'All the new children are to leave the coach first. Before you do so, please show me your hand baggage. Nothing is to be left on the bus! The girls will then please line up outside with Miss Thomas and the boys with Mr Johns. You will be shown to your dormitories and have a wash before dinner. Your main luggage will be sent upstairs later.'

Obediently, the new pupils queued up to leave the coach, showing Emma their hand baggage as they went. They were longing to get inside the building now, to see their new living quarters.

So, too, was Elizabeth. She waited impatiently for the last of the younger children to be ushered off the coach. She knew that she and Joan were to be in the same dormitory this year. But who would they be sharing with? And which room?

Just as their turn came to get off the coach, a small fair-haired boy reappeared and clambered back on board. He looked rather scared.

'Please, miss,' he said to Emma, blinking, 'I think I've left my teddy bear behind. I was sure it was in my carrier bag.'

'Don't look so frightened, Rupert!' replied the senior girl. 'We must try to find it quickly. We can't keep Mr Johns waiting.'

Elizabeth glanced around the empty seats at the front. Suddenly she spotted a furry paw sticking out from under one of the seats.

'I can see it!' she laughed, diving forward to pick it up. 'It's fallen on the floor!'

She handed it to the grateful boy. What a dear little face he had, she thought. He looked a rather dreamy child.

'There you are, Rupert,' smiled Emma. 'Say thank you to Elizabeth. And my name's Emma, by the way.'

'Yes, miss.'

As the bewildered child ran to join the other new juniors, Emma turned to Elizabeth with a gentle laugh. How pretty she looked when she laughed! thought Elizabeth. And how clever of her to have memorised the boy's name already. There were so many new ones this term.

'Well spotted, Elizabeth,' she said. 'I think we're all going to have to keep a motherly eye on Rupert. He's rather young for his age.'

'He thinks you're a teacher, Emma!'

'He'll soon find out that I'm just an ordinary pupil, like him,' laughed the senior girl.

Elizabeth gave Joan a meaningful glance.

They disembarked.

'I very much hope that Emma won't be an ordinary pupil for much longer!' she said. 'Don't you, Joan?'

'Yes, she's certainly got my vote!' agreed Joan.

'I can't understand why Jenny thinks Nora

might be better!' complained Elizabeth.

To their delight, the two friends found that they had been put in Room 14. And they were sharing with Jenny and Kathleen.

'What a lovely sunny room!' exclaimed Elizabeth. She ran to the window. 'And look at the view! We can see right across the grounds. Does anybody want this bed in the corner, or can I have it?'

'I like this one by the door,' said Kathleen.

'And I'm happy with this one by the window,' said Jenny good-naturedly.

The four girls went off to the bathrooms to wash and tidy up before dinner. When they got back to Room 14, they found their luggage waiting for them. It had been brought up from the coach.

'What's in your tuck box. Elizabeth?' asked Kathleen, hungrily. 'Let's see!'

Elizabeth showed them the big chocolate cake that she'd brought from home, to be shared out at teatime.

'I know I'll be starving again by then!' she said happily. 'I'm going to practise my table tennis this afternoon, after we've unpacked. If I can find someone to practise with!'

Second formers were eligible to play table tennis and to be chosen for school teams. Elizabeth had always loved the game and she knew she was good at it. She was pleased that she was old enough now to play it at Whyteleafe. She was longing to make one of the teams and play matches against other schools.

As they all looked in each other's tuck boxes, the four girls got hungrier and hungrier.

'That strawberry cake, Joan!' sighed Elizabeth. 'It's almost unbearable to look at it.'

'Mummy and I made it together,' said Joan proudly.

Luckily, before they could be tempted further, the dinner bell went.

'Hooray!'

In fact, it was the second dinner bell. They had somehow missed hearing the first one.

The girls raced downstairs to the dining hall, quickly realising that everybody else was already inside. Dinner was always served late on the first day of term, to allow time for all the pupils to get back. This made the boys and girls very hungry indeed. They knew there would be an extra special meal today, with plenty of delicious meat and gravy and fresh vegetables from the school gardens. No wonder all the other pupils had got there early.

'What kept you?' frowned Julian. There was a strange look on his face.

He had saved Elizabeth and Joan places at a big table by the window.

'What's the matter with you, Julian?' laughed Elizabeth. 'We didn't hear the first bell, that's all.'

But she quickly realised that there was something unusual afoot. All their classmates were in a huddle round the table, talking in low voices. Julian's cousin Patrick kept looking round, as though expecting something.

It wasn't just happening at their table, either.

An air of expectancy hung all around the dining hall.

'Whatever's going on, Julian?' she asked.

'I've had a horrible shock, Elizabeth.' There was still that funny expression on Julian's face. 'You and Joan are going to get one, too. You'll never guess in a thousand years!'

'Sssh!' said Patrick, rather bossily. 'Keep your voices down! You know we've been told not to make a fuss. Mr Leslie says we are all to behave perfectly normally.'

'Just because somebody's famous, they don't want to be stared and gawped at,' said Arabella, primly. In fact her hands were shaking slightly as she folded her napkin. She seemed hardly able to control her excitement. 'Mr Leslie's just been over to our table and had a word with us about it.'

'Famous?' asked Elizabeth. She settled down in her seat between Julian and Joan. 'What's being famous got to do with anything, Julian?'

'Look for yourself, Elizabeth,' he muttered, as the doors swung open. 'Look who's here!'

The three friends were facing the swing doors. They had a perfect view as an elegant figure swept into the dining hall, her golden hair brushed to a gleaming halo, her smile radiant. It was a grand entrance. Miss Belle and Miss Best, the joint headmistresses, bustled the girl quickly across to the senior pupils' table. A boy called Paul was already on his feet, pulling out a chair for her.

All round the dining hall, conversation ceased.

The clatter of knives and forks was stilled.

'What's *she* doing here?' whispered Elizabeth, indignantly. 'And whatever does she think she's doing wearing our school uniform? I don't understand!'

It was Kerry Dane.

4   *Elizabeth shows restraint*

'Elizabeth, can't you guess?' asked Julian. He tried not to laugh. The expression on Elizabeth's face was really comical!

The chatter in the dining hall had suddenly resumed, on a rather forced note, as the children remembered that they were supposed to take no notice of the new arrival and on no account to be rude and stare! It was a tall order but they were managing it well, even the younger ones. Two exceptions, at the second form table, were Patrick and Arabella. In spite of their fine words, they had actually swivelled round to get a better look. Patrick's eyes were almost out on stalks.

Elizabeth lowered her gaze and busily piled vegetables on to her plate. She was trying to collect her thoughts. What an astonishing turn of events! For a moment, in her bewilderment, she'd wondered if a scene for some new film was being shot at Whyteleafe School. But a quick glance towards the seniors' table showed no sign of cameras, or cameramen, or special lighting . . . It was every bit a real-life happening.

Kerry Dane, golden-haired, elegant in a brand new Whyteleafe uniform, was sitting with the other seniors, chatting, smiling, making friends . . .

'She's a new senior pupil, Elizabeth, that's what!' Julian was whispering. 'I'm very much afraid she's come to Whyteleafe! She must have been in that taxi which passed us. She must have been somewhere on our train.'

'So *that*'s why she was in such a rush this morning!' realised Joan, with a slight gasp. She, like Elizabeth, could hardly believe her eyes. The vision from the silver screen, the girl they had queued up to meet in London that morning, who had turned out to be such a disappointment, was sitting in this very dining hall. She was now a member of their school. 'She had to catch the train. The same train as us!'

Elizabeth glowered.

'Just look at her now!' She tossed her curls in the direction of the senior table. Kerry was talking animatedly to her new friends. 'If only they knew what she's really like!'

Julian grinned. He hissed from behind his hand:

'She'd have a surprise if she knew where those flowers were now!'

'Not as big a surprise as Mummy must have had when Daddy brought them home! Mummy does love flowers so!' replied Elizabeth, cheering up.

The three friends started to laugh.

'Hey, pass the roast potatoes please, Elizabeth.' That was Harry's voice. 'What are you three laughing and whispering about?'

'Oh, nothing!' Elizabeth said quickly.

'Isn't it wonderful that she's decided to come here?' Belinda was exclaiming. 'Of all the boarding schools her parents could have chosen, they chose Whyteleafe. I feel so proud.'

'It's going to be good for the school,' chimed in Kathleen, her rosy cheeks dimpling. 'And she's so nice. Wasn't she good in that film? Did you see it, Elizabeth?'

'Yes,' replied Elizabeth, at the same time giving both Julian and Joan a warning nudge.

Her feelings were still very raw. So far, the three friends had kept quiet about their adventure. And Elizabeth wanted to keep it that way. She wasn't going to tell her classmates about the humiliating episode in London. It had been such a horrible experience, asking Kerry Dane for an autograph!

But there was something else, too.

She knew that if she didn't guard her tongue carefully she would soon be rude about Kerry Dane. And they would think her very catty. At the moment, everybody believed that Kerry must be like Zara in the film. Elizabeth had believed that herself. They would find out soon enough, but this, reasoned Elizabeth, was hardly a good time to start upsetting her classmates. They were planning to elect her as a monitor at the end of the week!

'So what did you think, Elizabeth?' pressed Kathleen.

'She's a very good actress,' replied Elizabeth. 'Brilliant, I'd say.'

Julian was amused.

It was not often that the Naughtiest Girl showed such restraint. She really *was* on her best behaviour. She must want to be a second form monitor very badly!

After dinner, as soon as the three friends came out of the hall, Elizabeth gave full vent to her feelings.

'I don't feel in the least bit proud that she's come to Whyteleafe!' she declared. 'I wish she hadn't bothered! Why didn't she want to stay on at her London school? After all, she must be in the middle of studying for her certificate. It's a funny time to change schools.'

'Why go back to school at all, after you've been in a film and become famous?' wondered

Joan. 'You'd think she'd want to leave school now and try to be a full-time actress.'

'Perhaps she's not quite old enough to leave school,' Elizabeth pointed out. 'Or perhaps her parents think she should take her exams first.'

'But why Whyteleafe?' mused Julian, pushing his untidy black fringe back. He was puzzled. 'Why not some big famous school somewhere, with its own theatre and all that sort of thing. Somewhere really posh. We're only a small school, buried away in the countryside!'

Elizabeth thought this over carefully. As far as she was concerned, Whyteleafe was the best school in the whole world. But it was a fair point.

'You're right, Julian. Somehow Kerry Dane and Whyteleafe School just don't go together.'

'Perhaps she wants to be a big fish in a small pond?' suggested Joan, gently.

'She certainly wants to be noticed,' said Julian, shrewdly. 'That warning from Mr Leslie about how she wants to be treated like any other pupil and not made a fuss of . . . Really!

So why didn't she just slip quietly into the dining hall at the same time as the other seniors?'

'Yes! Why didn't she? Instead of making a grand entrance!' Elizabeth could feel a temper coming on. 'She wants to be the centre of attention, all right. She doesn't belong here. I'm longing for everyone to find out how horrible she is and then perhaps she'll go away again!'

'But we must let them find out for themselves, Elizabeth,' said Joan, quietly. 'You've decided that, haven't you? At the moment I don't think anyone would believe us if we told them what she's really like.'

'Don't worry, Joan.' Elizabeth linked arms with her friend. She had instantly calmed down. 'I know I mustn't lose my temper or say anything silly. But I've just thought of something – you don't think she might recognise me, do you? That would be a bit awkward!'

'She won't recognise *any* of us,' declared Julian, who had been thinking about it. 'We were wearing raincoats over our school uniform. There was nothing to connect us with Whyteleafe at all. And she certainly wouldn't recognise *you*, Elizabeth. Your hair was all plastered down by the rain. As a matter of fact, you looked a sight! Anyway, she didn't even bother to look at you.'

'Thank you, Julian,' said Elizabeth. What a mean, horrid person the girl was. Oh, her lovely autograph book! All spoiled now.

But she felt relieved, all the same. She had to make sure that she continued to keep her temper. It would make life very much simpler if Kerry Dane did not recognise her.

'I still find it odd, her coming to Whyteleafe, though,' mused Julian. 'You put it exactly, Elizabeth. She doesn't belong. Whyteleafe and Kerry Dane just don't mix. But now,' he continued airily, 'let's forget all about her, shall we? There's Harry looking for me. Isn't it time we all went and unpacked?'

'It certainly is,' agreed Joan. 'Come on, Elizabeth.'

Elizabeth needed no second bidding. Kerry Dane or no Kerry Dane, she was going to get on with her life! She was a second former now. She had a lovely new room. She was longing to get her things out of her trunk and arrange them just how she wanted. After that, she would go and practise her table tennis and work up an appetite for tea.

Her mouth watered at the thought of the delicious chocolate cake in her tuck box.

And Kathleen had some excellent news for them.

It was to do with the choosing of the new heads of school.

5 Julian is puzzled about something else

'You'll be pleased when you hear my news, Elizabeth,' said Kathleen, as she came into Room 14. 'I've been talking to some of the seniors and looking at the noticeboard.'

Joan smiled gently.

'I don't want to sound too monitor-ish, Kathleen, but you should have been up here unpacking. You know it's all got to be done by three o'clock.'

'Sorry, Joan!'

Jenny had unpacked her trunk already and left the room. Elizabeth and Joan had almost finished. Elizabeth was standing back and admiring the way she had arranged her ornaments and photograph frames. It was very satisfying to have been given a much larger chest of drawers this year and to be allowed to put extra things on top. How glad she was to be a second former now.

'What news, Kathleen?' she asked.

'It looks as though your wish is going to come true, Elizabeth,' smiled the rosy-cheeked girl. 'You know, what we were discussing on the train. It looks very likely that Thomas and Emma will be the new head-boy and head-girl.'

'How do you know?' Elizabeth asked eagerly.

She and Joan exchanged delighted looks.

'There's a notice up about it!' explained Kathleen. 'And their names have been written up there. Some of the seniors are backing them. And there are no other names up at all!'

Elizabeth clapped her hands with pleasure.

They'd all been sure that Thomas would be made head-boy. But – how pleasing – some of the top class agreed with her about Emma!

'Great minds think alike!' she said, gleefully. 'Oh, I think Emma's going to make a very fine head-girl.'

'So we may not even need an election then!' said Joan, happily. 'If no more names are put up Thomas and Emma will just be appointed the new head-boy and girl on Saturday and take the first Meeting.'

Now that William and Rita had left, Joan could think of no two nicer heads. As a monitor, she was looking forward to working with them and helping them in the running of the school.

And so was Elizabeth.

Knowing that she was going to be chosen as a monitor at the Meeting, she could hardly wait for Saturday to arrive.

She hummed happily to herself as she looked for her table-tennis bat. She would go and take a look at that notice herself sometime!

'And there are no other names up, Kathleen?' she asked. 'You're sure?'

'Quite sure!' laughed Kathleen.

Elizabeth spent the afternoon practising her table tennis. She had three quite even games with Patrick and then a long session with Harry. She found that she was able to beat Harry easily!

By the end, he was quite out of breath. A

few people had gathered to watch them.

'I'm going off to have a shower now!' he told Elizabeth, as he left. 'You're a great player, though. I'm really impressed.'

'I'm impressed, too,' said a quiet voice.

A senior girl had stepped forward. Elizabeth spun round to see who had spoken. It was Emma!

'I think you might be school team material, Elizabeth,' she said. 'I'm running some coaching sessions this term. Would you like to put your name down?'

'Oh, I'd love to!' replied Elizabeth eagerly, hardly able to believe her ears. 'Thank you, Emma.'

'If you come with me, I'll show you the list.'

The senior girl led Elizabeth along to the main school noticeboard. Proudly she signed up for the table-tennis coaching sessions.

'Oh, good. The first one's tomorrow!' she exclaimed.

But she realised that Emma was staring rather dreamily at the notice next to it. She followed Emma's gaze.

There it was, just as Kathleen had said:

APPOINTMENT OF HEAD-BOY
AND HEAD-GIRL

Pupils in the second form and above may propose names. Please write the candidate's name in block capitals, with the name of the proposer in brackets. *Do not put anyone's name forward unless you have first obtained their permission.* IF MORE THAN ONE NAME IS PUT FORWARD FOR EITHER POST, AN ELECTION WILL TAKE PLACE ON SATURDAY IN TIME FOR THE FIRST MEETING OF TERM.

The notice was signed by Miss Belle and Miss Best, the joint headmistresses of Whyteleafe School. There were only two names entered:

EMMA GLOVER [John Terry]
THOMAS HILL [Philippa Dearing]

Elizabeth smiled.

'Some of us were really hoping you might be made head-girl!' she blurted out. 'With Thomas as head-boy! It's really good that it seems to be all decided!'

'Oh, I wouldn't say that, Elizabeth,' replied Emma lightly, a flush coming to her cheeks. She was feeling very excited but was trying her best to hide it. 'I was very honoured when John and some of the others asked me if I would allow my name to go forward. But there's plenty of time for other names yet. There may have to be an election.'

'I'm sure there won't be!' said Elizabeth, confidently. 'Everybody in the school respects John and Philippa's opinions. I shouldn't think anyone would want to go against them. I know I certainly shan't.'

'Thank you, Elizabeth,' said Emma. 'And I'll see you tomorrow, then? I think I can help you a bit with that service.'

Feeling extremely pleased with life, Elizabeth went off to find John Terry. He was one of her favourite people at Whyteleafe. He was in charge of the school gardens and she knew that was where she would find him.

'Hello, Elizabeth!' he greeted her. He straightened up, trowel in hand. 'Look at what all the weeds have been doing while we've been away! Happy to be back, then?'

'Very!' said Elizabeth. 'And even happier that you've persuaded Emma to stand as head-girl. Won't she make a fine one?'

'Some of us think so,' he said.

'Only some of you?' asked Elizabeth.

'Well, there are those that are worried that she's not forceful enough. I don't agree with them.'

'Nor do I!' said Elizabeth.

'But a few of them *are* worried.'

'Like Jenny then,' laughed Elizabeth. 'She says the same thing. But it's silly, isn't it?'

John nodded, wisely, and returned to his weeding.

At teatime, Elizabeth was told that Jenny had

gone along to see Nora. She had gone to ask her permission to put her name forward as head-girl.

'What did she say?' asked Elizabeth, when Jenny appeared.

'She refused,' said Jenny, with a sigh. 'She said she doesn't feel she can stand in Emma's way. Isn't that noble of her? Now I don't suppose there will be an election at all. It might have been fun. I was looking forward to it!'

'Well, never mind, Jenny,' said Elizabeth. 'She would have lost anyway. Want a piece of chocolate cake? Doesn't it look scrumptious?'

Teatime on the first day back was always very enjoyable. The children were permitted to bring their tuck boxes to the dining hall and share some of the good things that they'd brought from home. They were allowed to go and chat to people at other tables. There was quite an informal atmosphere on the first day of term.

'Kerry Dane was with Nora when I went to see her,' Jenny confided, watching hungrily as

Elizabeth divided up the cake. 'They seem to be quite friendly. She's really nice, you know. She's *just* like Zara in the film. She asked me all about myself.'

'Yes, everybody's saying how nice she is!' agreed Belinda.

'Hurry up with that cake, Elizabeth!' said Julian. He had been out all afternoon, helping Robert with the school ponies. 'It looks very good.'

'Wait a minute, Julian!' scolded Elizabeth. She had counted the number of children at the table. She wanted them each to have a piece. 'I'm trying to get the slices all exactly the same size.'

While completing this task, Elizabeth became aware of a sudden buzz of excitement around the table. She looked up, quickly.

Kerry Dane had just strolled into the dining hall, arm in arm with Nora. They were heading this way! Kerry was giving Jenny a friendly little wave.

'Hello, Jenny!' she said, as she reached the

table. 'You promised to introduce me to some of the second formers. So here I am!'

There was a moment's awe-struck silence. The radiant, golden-haired 'Zara' was in their midst! For a split-second, Elizabeth herself was affected by it. Even without make-up, and wearing just an ordinary Whyteleafe uniform, Kerry Dane had a mesmerising presence. She really did have star quality.

'What a lovely spread!' she said as she gazed round at the open tuck boxes. 'Nobody told me that we could bring things in. I haven't got a tuck box!' she added, screwing up her eyes and pretending to sob. 'Why didn't anybody tell me?'

The children laughed. The young star certainly knew how to put them at their ease! Soon they were all talking at once, introducing themselves. Jenny, flushed with pride at the unexpected visit, offered Kerry some shortbread.

'Do you like popcorn?' Patrick was asking eagerly.

But now Kerry had turned and walked over to Elizabeth.

Elizabeth froze, her head lowered as she pretended to divide up the cake, though in fact the task was complete. She drew in a sharp breath.

The moment had come. Would Kerry Dane recognise her?

'Hello!' Kerry was saying. 'Nora tells me you're Elizabeth, otherwise known as the Naughtiest Girl in the school.' She gave a friendly little laugh. 'But that you're really one of our best pupils. A completely reformed character!'

Steeling herself, Elizabeth looked up and met Kerry's gaze full on. But she need not have worried. Julian's surmise had been correct.

There was not a flicker of recognition.

Kerry had no idea that the two of them had met that morning, in such very different circumstances! Already her gaze was falling from Elizabeth's face to her real interest – the lovely big chocolate cake. And her mouth was watering.

'How do you do,' said Elizabeth politely.

'I would do very well with a piece of that gorgeous cake. I'm afraid chocolate is my great weakness!' replied the star, sweetly. 'Can you spare a piece?'

She was looking full into Elizabeth's eyes again, willing her to agree. In the electric silence between them, Elizabeth could feel the invisible force of that will. Kerry Dane wanted a piece of the chocolate cake. And whatever Kerry Dane wanted, must be given to her.

'I'm sorry,' Elizabeth replied, meeting that fierce gaze. 'I'm afraid it's all spoken for.'

For a fraction of a second, a cold hardness crossed Kerry's face, the exact look that Elizabeth had seen before. For that brief moment, the mask slipped and the real Kerry Dane showed through.

'Oh, Elizabeth, how mean!' Arabella was exclaiming. 'You can have my piece, Kerry—'

'No, have mine,' Patrick added.

'No, mine!' said Martin.

As some of the boys and girls clamoured for the privilege of giving up their slice of chocolate cake, Kerry turned and faced them, at her most charming once again.

'I wouldn't dream of letting any of you give me your cake!' she smiled. 'How silly of me to ask! Really greedy of me. Nora will take me over to our own table and we'll see what's on offer there! But before we go—'

She looked directly at Jenny.

'There's something Nora wants to say to you, Jenny. I think you're going to be pleased.'

Elizabeth, Joan and Julian exchanged surprised looks. For the first time they realised that Nora, usually a calm, sensible person, had a rather silly over-excited expression on her face.

'If you really think I would make a good head-girl, Jenny,' said Nora, her cheeks flushed, 'then I will let my name go forward, after all. I might as well.'

'Oh, good!' exclaimed Jenny, although she was rather taken aback. Less than ten minutes earlier, Nora had been so definite about not standing. 'I'm so pleased, Nora. I'll go and put your name up after tea. Oh, what fun! We'll be able to have a proper election now.'

'Always the fairest way,' smiled Kerry Dane. 'I do think Nora's made the right decision. She's told me how important the post is. The more candidates the better! May the best girl win!' she added lightly.

Elizabeth ground her teeth.

'I hate her!' she said to Julian and Joan, later. 'What does she know about our school? It's not a bit fair of her to flatter poor Nora like that.'

'Yes,' agreed Joan. 'I think you're right and that's what's happened. She must have talked Nora into standing. Against her better judgement.'

'And she's bound to get beaten,' nodded Elizabeth. 'If any of the seniors really wanted Nora, they would have put her name up themselves. It's obvious they've decided they want Emma.'

'But it's not just the seniors who vote,' Julian pointed out. 'I think we should run an election campaign for Emma, don't you? Just to help her on her way!'

'Oh, Julian, what an excellent idea!' exclaimed Elizabeth. 'We can make a banner. And we can get Belinda to do some posters. She's good at art!'

'I think your idea's a very good one, Julian,' said Joan, after due thought. 'The whole school is so taken in by Kerry Dane, the very fact that she approves of there being an election will tend to bring Nora a few votes. We must do all we can to help Emma.'

'The whole school won't be taken in much longer!' declared Elizabeth, confidently. She was feeling cheerful again. 'Kerry Dane won't be able to keep up her act of being like Zara in the film for ever! Did you see the way the mask slipped when I wouldn't give her any chocolate cake? Greedy pig! Did you see the look she gave me?'

'Well, no, she had her back to the rest of us,' said Julian, looking amused. 'I can imagine it, though! But I was right about her not recognising you, wasn't I, Elizabeth?'

'Yes, Julian!' laughed Elizabeth. 'You were right as usual!'

The three friends set off for the art and crafts room, eager to start the preparations for Emma's election campaign.

As they walked along, Julian dug his hands in his pockets, deep in thought. He was frowning slightly.

'There's something that puzzles me about Kerry Dane.'

'You mean, why she's come to a little school like ours?' asked Elizabeth. 'Yes, it is puzzling.'

'Well, that, of course. But something else. Why should she work on Nora and get her to stand for head-girl?'

'Well, she's probably jealous of Emma for being so nice,' volunteered Joan.

'But if you ask me,' said Julian, darkly. 'What she'd *really* like is to be head-girl herself.'

The two girls looked at Julian in surprise.

'She's new. She can't be!' exclaimed Elizabeth. 'Oh, Julian, what a ridiculous idea!'

6 The naughtiest girl wants to win

'Good morning, children,' said Mr Leslie, the next day, 'and welcome to the second form all of you who have come up this term. Please find yourselves a desk and get settled down. Then I'll give out the new timetable.'

Elizabeth stared round her new form room with pleasure. It was large and airy with windows on two sides. Those pupils already in the second form, like Joan and Jake and Howard, were seated back at their old desks. The rest of them, from the first form, had to find their own.

'Can we really sit anywhere we like, Joan?' whispered Elizabeth, making straight for the empty desk next to her friend's. 'When I first arrived in the first form we had to remain standing until Miss Ranger told us where to go.'

'You're a second former now, Elizabeth!' laughed Joan.

Elizabeth felt very pleased as she settled down next to Joan. Carefully she stacked her books in her desk. It was true. She really *was* in the second form at last. And very soon now – after this week's Meeting – she would be a second form monitor!

She was going to enjoy having Mr Leslie as her class teacher, although she would miss Miss Ranger, of course. She was also going to enjoy having a new timetable and learning new things. But most of all she was going to enjoy the Meetings and being a monitor with Joan. They would sit on the platform each week, as second form representatives, with all the other monitors. They would sit in a row, just behind the new head-boy and girl.

Whyteleafe was a very unusual school. It was largely governed by the children themselves. The weekly Meetings were like a school parliament, where problems were discussed and grievances aired. When any cases of wrongdoing were reported to the Meeting it then became more like a court, with the monitors as the jury and the head-boy and girl as the judges. Miss Belle and Miss Best, the joint head-mistresses, sat in on the Meetings, together with Mr Johns, the senior master, but they were mere observers. It was left to the pupils themselves to decide how things should be dealt with.

And Thomas was going to make an excellent head-boy, Elizabeth felt. He could be relied upon to be totally fair, as William had been. Emma would be just the same, as head-girl; she was truly worthy to step into Rita's shoes. Oh, they must make absolutely certain that it *was* Emma who became head-girl, now there was to be an election!

'You are not to lose your new timetables,' said Mr Leslie, as Joan handed them round the class. 'There's just one each and none left over!'

Elizabeth stuck hers down inside the front cover of her rough book. She studied it carefully. They were going to have more science lessons this year, with Mr Leslie. And more

French with Mamselle. There were to be more games lessons, too. And they would still have Miss Ranger for English. Good! She would be able to choose between various outdoor sports this term. And on rainy days they'd be allowed, during games lessons, to play either chess or table tennis.

Table tennis. Hurray! thought Elizabeth. *I do hope I get in a team!*

After school today Emma would be holding the first coaching session. Elizabeth was looking forward to it eagerly.

But, before that, there was something else to look forward to.

The three friends had been very busy in the craft room last night. They had made a beautiful banner. Julian had fixed it to a light wooden frame, so that someone could hold it aloft and march along with it.

At dinner time, the election campaign could begin in earnest. And so it did.

'Roll up, roll up!' shouted Julian, his hands cupped to his mouth. 'Join on the end if you support us. Roll up! Roll up!'

Julian stood by the open doors as boys and girls emerged from dinner. He was shouting encouragement.

It was a merry sight, as the Naughtiest Girl came marching on to the scene.

Elizabeth was striding this way, holding aloft a bright banner. It said:

VOTE FOR EMMA
EMMA FOR HEAD-GIRL!

With Harry banging a toy drum beside her and Joan just behind, they began to parade round the big sunny lawn. From the second form, Belinda and Kathleen quickly joined on. Then a gaggle of excited juniors, who all adored Emma, tagged on behind. They started singing at the tops of their voices: 'Roll up! Roll up for Emma . . .!'

Each time Elizabeth circled the lawn, the procession grew longer. Soon there were more than twenty pupils in the parade, while others stood round applauding. Some of them were seniors, like John Terry and Philippa Dearing. It was beneath their dignity to join the parade but they were happy to clap and cheer.

'Well done, Elizabeth!' John Terry called out, each time she marched past him.

When the bell went for afternoon lessons, Elizabeth and Julian returned the banner to a cupboard in the craft room.

'Wasn't that good, Julian!' said Elizabeth, her face flushed with excitement.

'Very!' His eyes glinted with amusement. 'Pity some of them aren't old enough to vote. But we've made a grand start!'

'We must do it every day until the election,' vowed Elizabeth. 'I'll ask Sophie to play the flute tomorrow! We'll remind people every day who they should vote for! And Belinda's promised to make posters later today.'

After school, Elizabeth collected her table-tennis bat and hurried to the coaching session. She was the first to arrive.

'I saw your parade at dinner time,' confessed

Emma. She looked very pleased, if slightly embarrassed. 'Elizabeth, I was very touched.'

'Nora hasn't got a chance!' replied Elizabeth, in her usual forthright way. 'We respect her but most of us think she's a bit too bossy to be head-girl!'

Emma quickly turned to hide a smile. And just at that moment, several other children arrived – including Julian's cousin, Patrick.

'Hello, Elizabeth,' he said, in surprise. 'I didn't know you'd put your name down for coaching.'

'Emma suggested it,' replied Elizabeth, sweetly.

Patrick frowned. He couldn't help liking Elizabeth but he was very competitive. It would be rather annoying if a girl – and especially the Naughtiest Girl – managed to bag a place in the table-tennis team ahead of him. Emma clapped her hands.

'Right, everyone. First of all, I'm going to go through Elizabeth's service action with her. She needs some help with it. I want you all to gather round the table and watch, in case there are some tips for the rest of you.'

By the end of the session, Elizabeth's service action had already improved. In spite of the fact that Emma had helped him with his forehand smash, Patrick was annoyed when Elizabeth managed to beat him 21–18 in a practice game.

'No wonder you want Emma to be head-girl,' he said, as they went off to tea.

'Patrick! How dare you? She helped us all equally!'

'Sorry! Sorry!' he said quickly, seeing the tempestuous look in Elizabeth's eye. 'Only joking.'

'I should think so,' replied Elizabeth. 'But honestly, Patrick, who else *could* be head-girl? Aren't you going to vote for her yourself?'

'I don't know yet. I'm not sure that she's got enough presence. But then I don't think Nora's quite right, either.'

'She's quite wrong!' replied Elizabeth witheringly.

* * *

After tea, Elizabeth helped Belinda put up her little posters round the school. She thought they were very effective. Written in large letters, in brightly-coloured crayons, were some simple slogans.

X
VOTE ON SATURDAY
X EMMA X

DON'T FORGET
XX EMMA XX

EMMA FOR HEAD
USE YOUR VOTE
X

'They're really eye-catching, Belinda,' said Elizabeth admiringly, as they fixed one to the door of the third form common room. 'Everybody's going to notice them!' She gave a little sigh. 'But I do wish Jenny hadn't put

Nora's name forward. It's unsettling, somehow, though she can't possibly win.'

'I agree,' replied Belinda. She surveyed her handiwork, feeling quite pleased with it. 'None of the boys wants to stand against Thomas. It's just taken for granted that he's going to be head-boy. But now Nora's standing against Emma, it's sort of raised doubts in people's minds. It's started lots of discussion and made them worry whether Emma will be forceful enough, even though they don't think Nora's right.'

'Yes,' said Elizabeth, 'it would have been better if Emma could have been elected unopposed. But as Jenny told me last night, nobody's got an exclusive right to be head-girl and they shouldn't be frightened of an election. It's a fair point. We've just got to make sure that Emma gets a huge vote on Saturday. On her merits! I'm sure she will! As a matter of fact, Belinda, I'm quite enjoying this election campaign.'

'Yes, it's fun!'

* * *

Going upstairs, at bedtime, Elizabeth smiled as she saw some tiny notices on doors. They were written in Jenny's handwriting. They said simply VOTE FOR NORA. She thought they looked rather feeble, compared with Belinda's efforts.

And when she got to Room 14, she found Jenny in a chastened mood.

'I'm not getting a lot of support for Nora,' she confessed, as the girls sipped their bedtime cocoa. 'I'm sure Kerry will vote for her and one or two other seniors. But I think she may only get about twenty votes altogether.'

'Serves you right, Jenny!' laughed Elizabeth.

Joan was gentler about it.

'Poor Jenny,' she said to Elizabeth, when they went with Kathleen to clean their teeth.

'And poor Nora!' added Kathleen.

'Yes,' agreed Elizabeth. *And it's all Kerry Dane's fault for interfering. What does she know about Whyteleafe School?*

Elizabeth was longing for Kerry's mask to

crack, for the rest of the school to see the young actress in her true colours. Only then could she tell her classmates about the adventure that she, Joan and Julian had had in London. And how the three of them had known all along that she was not nearly as nice as she seemed. That she was, in fact, perfectly horrid.

But three whole days passed by.

And, by Friday evening, Elizabeth was getting impatient.

'I don't know how Kerry Dane's managing to keep it up!' she complained to Julian, as they came indoors together after a ride on the ponies. 'She's so nice to everybody all the time, especially the older forms. Everybody thinks they're getting to know her properly. They keep saying she's even nicer than the part she played in the film. Really!'

'Yes. I hear she's offered to do something for the Earthquake Bazaar!' observed Julian. 'You know, the sale that the seniors are going to hold, to raise money for the earthquake victims. She's running the sweet stall, or something.

Arabella's been making some fudge for it.'

'I know,' said Elizabeth, grinding her teeth. '*And* she's offered to get someone important from the film world to come and open it. Everybody thinks she's marvellous! How *does* she keep it up? It must be a terrible strain for her. I simply can't think why she bothers.'

'Hallo!' said Julian suddenly, as he looked down the corridor. 'What's going on? There's quite a crowd round the noticeboard.'

Elizabeth and Julian hurried over and pressed forward to get a good look. There was a buzz of excited chatter all around them. Everybody was gazing at the election list for head-boy and girl.

Miss Belle and Miss Best would be taking the notice down tonight. But another name had been added, at the last moment!

A third nomination for head-girl had been added to the list. The name was written clearly, in a senior boy's bold handwriting:

KERRY DANE [Paul Kirk]

Elizabeth backed away from the noticeboard, laughing out loud in shock.

Julian whistled to himself.

'There's your answer, Elizabeth,' he said. 'All is explained.'

7   A very close result

Elizabeth listened to the babble of voices all around her. Everyone seemed to be talking at once. There were many conflicting opinions.

'Paul persuaded her! She shouldn't have listened to him!'

'She didn't really want to stand. She says she's too new.'

'And she is. Much too new! If she'd been here a while, and been a monitor, I'd definitely vote for her. She'd make a marvellous head-girl. But—'

'But why not? Paul says the important thing is just to get the very best person. If people were so sure about Emma, why would Nora bother to stand?'

'Yes! And seeing there's going to be an election *anyway* . . .'

'I say, wouldn't Hickling Green be envious if we had Kerry Dane for head-girl! They're such a lot of stuck-up snobs! And you know, I can just see her on the platform, taking the Meetings with Thomas. She's got such presence!'

'Yes, she has. But it wouldn't be right – it's got to be a real Whyteleafean. It's got to be Emma or Nora.'

'I agree with you, Candida!'

'Yes! I'll be voting for one of the old stagers.'

'Me, too. Emma, in fact . . .'

'But she *would* have made a marvellous head-girl.'

Elizabeth and Julian walked away.

'*A marvellous head-girl?*' exploded Elizabeth. 'She'd be a disaster! Oh, Julian, do you think she's been planning this?'

'I'm sure she has,' frowned Julian. 'From the moment she saw the chance to provoke an election and unsettle things. What a schemer!'

'Julian, you don't think . . .' The idea filled Elizabeth with horror. 'You don't think there are enough people who'd be *silly* enough . . . to get sort of carried away and vote for her on the spur of the moment? So that she ends up being elected?'

It was like looking into the abyss.

'There'll be some,' said Julian, thoughtfully. 'But not a majority, I'm quite sure. You heard what everyone was saying. Most people feel strongly that she's much too new. They may be dazzled by her but they are going to vote for Emma or Nora.'

'Good! Then we've got to make sure it's Emma!' said Elizabeth fervently. 'Let's have one last parade tomorrow, Julian. The best parade yet! Straight after breakfast. Just before the election!'

Voting was at ten the next morning. The School Meeting would follow at eleven.

At bedtime, Jenny looked unhappy.

'I am surprised,' she said, 'that Kerry's allowed her own name to go forward! She came to talk to me about it. She said she didn't want it to happen but other people were insisting.

And, after what she'd said to me about Nora standing, she couldn't really refuse, could she? But she told me not to worry. She's promised to vote for Nora herself, and she's going to tell everyone she meets to vote for Nora, as well! Isn't that sweet of her?'

Elizabeth didn't believe a word of it. But out loud she said, 'So what's the matter, then?'

'Oh, nothing!' Jenny replied quickly.

Jenny was too proud to admit to Elizabeth that Kerry Dane had forgotten her name already. She'd kept calling her Jane! It had left Jenny feeling rather uneasy. There was something odd about the whole thing but she couldn't quite put her finger on what it was.

Saturday morning dawned bright and sunny. The election campaign for Emma reached its climax. Elizabeth organised the final parade with great flair. Sophie came with her flute and all the juniors brought tambourines. And Richard agreed to strum his guitar! For the last hour before the voting began, Elizabeth marched her band around and around the outside of the school buildings, holding the banner aloft.

Each time they passed below dormitory windows, Harry banged the drum and Julian shouted, 'Wake up! Wake up! Don't forget to come and vote!'

And the juniors chorused, 'VOTE FOR EMMA! VOTE FOR EMMA! ROLL UP, ROLL UP AND VOTE FOR EMMA!'

Cheerful faces appeared at windows. There were smiles and waves.

Elizabeth found the whole thing very exhilarating. Afterwards, she said, 'I'm sure Emma's going to win, Joan. I just feel it in my bones!'

'Let's hope so,' replied Joan gently. 'At least there should be a good turnout now! Come on, Elizabeth. We mustn't forget to cast our *own* votes. It's nearly ten o'clock.'

Miss Belle and Miss Best were in charge of the election, which took place in the dining hall.

As Elizabeth joined the queue of people waiting to cast their vote, her confidence grew. What an excellent turnout! If most of these people were voting for Emma, then Kerry Dane was in for a big disappointment.

When she reached the head of the queue, Miss Belle ticked her name off a list and Miss Best handed her a voting paper. Elizabeth then walked through to a special table, picked up one of the pencils there and firmly marked a cross against Emma's name. As she carefully folded her ballot paper, she squinted along the table and saw that a third former was marking his cross in the same place. Good!

Under the watchful eye of the joint headmistresses, Elizabeth posted her voting slip into the big ballot box. It was a very satisfying feeling, to have cast her vote. The Beauty and the Beast, as the children called the heads, both smiled at her warmly.

'I wonder if they know I'm going to be made a monitor today?' wondered Elizabeth. 'I seem to be in their good books.'

She met up with Joan and Julian outside the hall and the three friends wandered along to their common room together. Some fourth formers, walking along the corridor ahead of them, were talking loudly.

'I was going to vote for Kerry,' one of them was saying, 'but I changed my mind this morning. Kerry persuaded me to vote for Nora. She's just so positive she'd be best!'

'Oh, how funny. She said something to me, too. She's very persuasive, isn't she! I really had to fight with myself to stick to my guns and vote for Emma.'

'Isn't it decent of her not to expect people to vote for her but to ask them to vote for Nora instead?'

The three friends heard this in some surprise.

'So it's true, then!' said Elizabeth. 'Jenny told me that Kerry had promised to campaign for Nora. I didn't believe she really would.'

'How very odd,' said Joan.

Julian said nothing. He looked worried.

'Well at least Kerry Dane can't possibly win

herself now!' declared Elizabeth.

While the votes were being counted in the hall, all the boys and girls had morning break. Then they went to their rooms to get spruced up for the Meeting. Elizabeth was in a state of high excitement by now.

Kathleen came and brushed some fluff off the collar of her blazer for her. She was smiling and rosy-cheeked as usual.

'Well, the suspense will soon be over!' she said. 'I'm sure Emma will have won. And we know Thomas has, because nobody stood against him. And then we'll be able to get on with all the proper business of the Meeting. You're still quite happy about being a monitor again, Elizabeth?'

'Kathleen, need you ask!' exclaimed Elizabeth, with a happy laugh.

The Meeting had arrived at last. She was looking forward to it.

They filed into the school hall and took up their new places on the second form benches. Elizabeth sat next to Julian. Joan left them and took her place up on the platform, with the other monitors. The hall was filling up very quickly. Elizabeth glanced across to the senior benches. Emma was sitting there, next to John and Philippa. Kerry Dane was sitting beside Paul, her hair brushed to a beautiful golden sheen.

At the back of the hall sat Mr Johns and the Beauty and the Beast, as always, although they would take no part in the Meeting.

When everybody was seated, Thomas walked into the hall.

A cheer went up as the tall, fair-haired boy mounted the platform and stood behind the special head-boy and girl's table. He held up his hand for silence. In his other hand, he held a piece of paper.

The election results!

A hush descended over the hall as Thomas started to speak. Elizabeth realised that she was clenching her hands into tight little fists and that her heart was beating faster than usual.

'I am very proud to be the new head-boy of

Whyteleafe School,' he told them, in his clear, pleasant voice. There was a deadpan expression on his face. It gave nothing away. 'And now, without further ado, I am going to read out the results of the election for our new head-girl. She will then be able to take her place on the platform beside me and the business of the Meeting can commence.'

He opened up the piece of paper. Elizabeth held her breath.

'The number of votes cast for each candidate was as follows: Nora – 29 votes. Emma – 34 votes. Kerry – 35 votes.'

Elizabeth gasped. Was she having a bad dream?

Thomas was giving a signal to someone on the senior benches.

'I declare Kerry Dane the new head-girl. Would you come up on to the platform, please, Kerry? And would everybody give Kerry a round of applause, please.'

The school buzzed with surprise and then began clapping.

What a close result! It could hardly have been closer. But as Kerry ran lightly up to the platform, many of the first formers and juniors looked crestfallen. They had never seen Kerry Dane's film. She was such a remote figure to them – not like Emma.

Elizabeth turned and looked at Julian in disbelief.

'It isn't possible,' she whispered, in horror.

Julian was busily doing some calculations on his fingers.

'I'm afraid it is, Elizabeth,' he whispered back. 'How very clever of her. Very cunning indeed.'

Elizabeth tossed her head. She wasn't listening. She was glancing across at Emma. The senior girl was trying to smile but was fighting back the tears. It would have been such a privilege, such an honour, to serve Whyteleafe School as its head-girl. She had so longed to be chosen. John Terry placed an arm round her shoulders to comfort her. There was an angry expression on his face.

Suddenly Elizabeth was incandescent with rage. Her temper boiled over.

She got to her feet.

'It's not fair! I don't know what's happened but it's not fair!' she hissed at Julian. 'I'm going!'

She marched off towards the exit.

Julian didn't hesitate. He jumped up and followed her. 'Me, too, Elizabeth,' he said, catching her up.

Trembling and upset, Joan scraped her chair back and left the platform with quiet dignity.

With Elizabeth leading the way, the three friends walked out of the Meeting.

8   New monitors have to be found

'Silence, please, everyone,' said Thomas, banging loudly on the table with the gavel that William and Rita had always used. 'Will you settle down at once and pay attention?'

It was Thomas's first big test as head-boy. The hall was in something of an uproar. The Naughtiest Girl had marched out of the Meeting, with two of her friends! What a surprise.

Thomas could have turned to the Beauty and the Beast for advice but he had no intention of doing so. He must handle this himself. He thought hard about what William or Rita would have done. They would have handled it with a light touch. He must follow suit.

'That's better,' he smiled, as the Meeting came to order. 'I'm afraid that elections can make people very emotional sometimes, especially when the result is extremely narrow. Let us take no notice of what has happened. Elizabeth and her friends will soon calm down and come back to join us. But now I want the Meeting to get straight down to business . . .'

However, Kerry Dane had other ideas. She was not going to be deprived of her moment of glory by those three people walking out, or by Thomas wanting to get on with the silly Meeting. She had a speech all prepared!

'First of all, I'd like to say a few words, if I may, Thomas.'

She walked forward to the very front of the platform. She felt exultant, as she stood before the assembled school, her beautiful hair making a halo of golden light around her head. It felt so right, somehow, that she, Kerry Dane, should be up here, with all those faces gazing at her. Now she was mistress of all she surveyed. This was what she was used to, ever since becoming famous. This was how it should be!

'I want to tell you all how humble I feel,' she

began. 'I never, ever dreamt of being elected. I never expected an honour like this. You had two such fine candidates for the position of head-girl. I am merely a new girl. I am so proud that, in spite of this, I am the person who has been elected – and I promise to serve Whyteleafe School to the very best of my ability. Thank you.'

The children listened, mesmerised.

She made an impressive sight and it was an impressive little speech.

There was applause. Patrick, Arabella and Martin exchanged smug looks. They had all voted for Kerry, and some of their classmates had criticised them. How wrong they were. Even the first formers and juniors began to feel more cheerful. Kerry seemed a nice person. They would just have to get used to not having Emma as head-girl . . .

Kerry stood there, acknowledging the applause. She was in a happy state, wanting it to go on and on.

The applause was dying away now with only

the die-hards like Arabella continuing to clap.

But still Kerry stood there.

'Ahem,' said Thomas, politely. 'Time to start, Kerry.'

She seemed not to hear.

Looking a little cross, Thomas had to bang the gavel again to bring the Meeting to order. Only then did the newly-elected head-girl come and take her seat beside him. She had almost forgotten where she was.

'Right, first things first,' Thomas told the Meeting. 'Will you all give your money in, please? Richard will come round with the school box.'

Kerry Dane watched in surprise as the wooden box was passed along the rows. Into the box went all the money that the children had brought back from home after the summer holidays.

'At Whyteleafe School,' Thomas explained to the new pupils below, 'it is not thought fair for some children to have more money than others. You will find that at every Meeting, any money you've been sent will be collected up. After that, each child in the school receives two pounds pocket money for the week. You are then allowed to make Special Requests if you need extra money for something important. Every request is listened to carefully and then the Meeting decides.'

While the box was going round, Kerry pulled out her wallet and counted the banknotes inside. She saw Thomas glance at them.

'Obviously, Thomas,' said Kerry, sweetly, 'this rule doesn't apply to us? Not to the head-girl and head-boy of the school?'

'I'm afraid it does, Kerry,' he said tersely. 'Seniors do have more calls on their purse than the younger children, so you will find that no reasonable request is ever turned down. But in the meantime –' he looked at the banknotes hard '– all of those must go in the box.'

Kerry managed to conceal her shock. What a ridiculous system! She would have to find some way of getting round it.

In the meantime, when the box came to the

platform, she had no choice but to place all her money inside under Thomas's watchful gaze.

Soon, the week's pocket money had been handed out to every pupil in the school and it was time to hear Special Requests for extra funds.

Julian's cousin was one of the first on his feet.

'I think Patrick *should* be allowed the money for a new table-tennis bat, Thomas,' Kerry decided. 'He tells me he's a very keen player.'

She was beginning to enjoy herself again. It was lovely to have so much power over the other children. Some of them would find their requests refused, if she didn't like the look of their faces!

Thomas did not agree at all that Patrick needed a new table-tennis bat but he had to let it pass. Kerry obviously did not understand the rules about Special Requests. It would all have to be explained to her. Now Patrick had been given an unfair advantage over other children who were also hoping to get into Emma's table-tennis squad.

But it would not be right to have an argument with Kerry in front of the entire school. It would undermine her authority.

As more Special Requests came and went, Thomas was keeping an eye on the doors at the back. Surely the Naughtiest Girl would have cooled down by now? He very much hoped so.

She and her two friends should really come back to the Meeting quickly. He expected to see them slip quietly back into their seats and show that they had now accepted the verdict of the ballot box. However regrettable, thought Thomas, that verdict had turned out to be.

Elizabeth had raced off to the school vegetable gardens. When Julian and Joan caught her up, she was marching up and down one of the little paths.

She walked up and down like that for some minutes, in order to work off her temper.

When at last she grew tired, the three of them sat on a sunny bench, just in front of the greenhouses.

'Let's have an apple,' said Joan, in her gentlest voice.

She picked three rosy apples from one of the little trees nearby. They each took a bite. As Elizabeth tasted the sweet, sharp tang of the fruit, she gazed around sorrowfully. These dear gardens, how she loved them. How she loved helping John Terry with the weeding and planting and hoeing.

Dear Whyteleafe School, the best school in the entire world. What happy times she had had here. But now, surely, it could never be the same again?

'It's the worst thing that's ever been,' she said miserably. 'And how did it happen? I just don't understand. Emma seemed to have so much support. You were wrong for once, Julian! You were so sure that most of the school wouldn't vote for Kerry, however much they admired her.'

'I wasn't wrong at all,' replied Julian, patiently. 'You obviously haven't done your sums, Elizabeth. Most of the school did *not* vote for Kerry Dane. She only collected about one third of the vote. She always knew that would be the best she could hope for. That was why she got Nora to stand. And *that* was why she went round persuading people to vote for Nora.'

'You mean . . . ?' Elizabeth frowned, trying to work it out.

'Julian means that Kerry guessed that a majority would never vote to elect a new girl,' explained Joan. 'But if she could split that majority in two, as evenly as possible—'

'She could squeeze through the middle and maybe win!' finished Julian. 'And that's exactly what happened. It was a master stroke, begging people to vote for Nora. It made some of them worry about voting for Emma and change their minds. And it made *some* of them, who may have been thinking of voting for Emma, but who didn't have strong principles about not electing a new girl, think "I don't want to vote for Nora but what a fine person Kerry is. I shall give her my vote." So she picked up some extra votes for herself as she went along. That's what made all the difference!'

'She would never have had a chance, if she'd just stood against Emma,' sighed Joan. 'She would have been very soundly beaten. But, as it turned out, she was able to split the vote three ways. What an impossible schemer! I realised what she had done as soon as Thomas read the result out. I felt such contempt for her that I just had to leave the platform, even though a monitor should never do a thing like that. I just had to.'

'It's not fair,' exclaimed Elizabeth. 'It's horrific!'

Julian threw his apple core so it landed on John Terry's compost heap. Then he glanced at his watch.

'Should you two be sitting here?' he asked. 'The Meeting must be racing along. They'll be getting to the bit about the second form monitors soon.'

Joan and Elizabeth looked at one another.

'I'm not going back in there,' said Joan bravely.

'Nor me,' stated Elizabeth.

Her face crumpled and tears of anger came to her eyes.

'I don't want to be a monitor any more. Not with her as head-girl! I couldn't bear, as a matter of fact, ever to sit on the same platform as her!'

'Those are my feelings exactly, Elizabeth,' declared Joan.

'Now,' said Thomas, gazing around the hall, 'we come to the last business of the day.'

Complaints and Grumbles had been dealt with. There had only been two.

'We have to sort out the second form monitors,' he continued. 'As you know, you are allowed two. Joan is still in the second form and can remain as a monitor, if you so wish. Or you may elect a new person, if you prefer. Susan has gone up into the third form this term. So a new monitor will have to be chosen to take Susan's place. Do you want to choose one new monitor, or two? What have you decided, second formers?'

Belinda rose to her feet. It had been agreed that she would be the spokesperson for the form. It had also been agreed what she should say. The words were written on a piece of paper.

Her cheeks hot with embarrassment, Belinda glanced round to see if there was any sign of Elizabeth and Joan coming back. For the past few minutes she had been looking out for them constantly. But they had not returned to the Meeting.

'Well, Belinda?' prompted Thomas.

Feeling awkward, Belinda read out the prepared statement.

'We, in the second form, have agreed unanimously that we would like Joan to continue as a monitor for another term. For our other monitor, we are all of the same opinion. We would like to appoint Elizabeth.'

As she sat down a buzz of conversation ran

round the hall. The second form wanted Joan and Elizabeth as monitors. But both girls had walked out of the Meeting! This was going to be an unusual situation. What would happen now?

'Please!' said Arabella, putting her hand up.

'You wish to say something?' asked Kerry Dane eagerly, from the platform.

Arabella stood up. She was feeling outraged at the way that Elizabeth, Joan and Julian had walked out of the Meeting earlier. Just because their favourite hadn't won! The election had been fought fair and square and Kerry had won. She was going to make such a fine head-girl. Perhaps she would be able to get Arabella a part in a film one day. She had almost hinted as much! It was extremely horrid and rude of Elizabeth and the others to walk out like that.

'When we've chosen monitors before, they've always had to stand up at the Meeting and agree,' she pointed out. 'But how can we elect Elizabeth and Joan if they're not here?'

'Shut up and sit down, Arabella!' hissed Daniel, crossly.

'You know they've agreed,' whispered Belinda, looking anxious. 'You know Joan's agreed to stay on and Elizabeth wants to be the new one.'

'What do the rules say about it, Thomas?' Kerry asked sweetly. 'Is there anything written about it in the Book?'

The Book was a large volume that stood on the table between them. It contained a record of everything important that had happened at Meetings and the many rules that had been agreed upon over the passage of time. Together, Kerry and Thomas pored over the Book together and soon found what they needed. They discussed it briefly with the monitors behind them and then Thomas turned to face the school. He looked upset.

'It appears to be an established rule that people must be here to be elected. The Meeting also feels that Elizabeth and Joan have ruled themselves out by such bad behaviour. So we've decided that the second form must now choose two new monitors. First find out if your choices are willing to stand, then write both names on a piece of paper.' He handed Kerry some slips of paper to take down to the second formers. 'We shall then count the votes and have a result very quickly.'

When Elizabeth and Joan went into dinner later, they learnt that Belinda and Daniel had been elected in their place.

They accepted the news bravely. Both girls were determined never to sit on the same platform as Kerry Dane, or recognise her as head-girl in other ways.

'I expect next week's Meeting will have to decide on some sort of punishment for us,' Joan sighed to her friends, after dinner. 'It's a very serious offence to miss a whole Meeting.'

'See if I care!' pouted Elizabeth.

'I don't expect the Meeting will punish you two,' said Julian, airily. 'They'll decide that you've been punished enough by losing your monitorships. They'll have to find some punishment for me, of course.'

Julian dug his hands in his pockets. His green eyes glinted.

'Whatever it is, it'll be worth it! It was good to make a stand. I really enjoyed it.'

'Yes,' nodded Elizabeth. 'I didn't mean to lose my temper. But it was good to show her what we think of her.'

Julian smiled to himself, in spite of everything. Life was never dull with the Naughtiest Girl around.

At bedtime that night, Elizabeth discovered that Jenny was very upset.

'I feel it's all my fault, Elizabeth. I should never have asked Nora to stand! It's worked out all wrong. Much as I admire Kerry, I never expected her to be elected as head-girl. She just doesn't seem right for it.'

'She doesn't seem right for anything!' said Elizabeth coldly. She had no need to keep her feelings to herself any longer. 'She's really hateful. I'll tell you all about it some time. But

I expect you'll find out soon enough.'

'Really?' Jenny looked intrigued. She frowned. 'In a way, I suppose, she doesn't seem right here at Whyteleafe at all.'

Elizabeth felt tired after all the strains of the day. She climbed into bed. But it was nice that Jenny was beginning to see sense. She had already forgiven her.

'Kerry's completely wrong for Whyteleafe,' she said sleepily. 'What Julian and Joan and I can't understand is what she's doing here at all!'

9 *Emma speaks to Elizabeth*

It was wet on Sunday. Elizabeth spent much of the day practising her table tennis. She hung around the green tables downstairs, getting as many games as she could. Soon she had perfected the new service that Emma had taught her. She then went on to improve her forehand smash. Patrick was practising hard, too.

They'd both discovered there was to be a match next Saturday, a friendly against St Faith's. It would be the first fixture of the new school year. And Emma and Mr Warlow would be choosing the squad after this week's coaching session. Elizabeth was determined to get in the team!

She found the forehand smash particularly satisfying. She was still feeling angry and upset.

She had left Joan sitting in the common room, hard at work with some knitting. Joan had decided to make a child's scarf for the Earthquake Bazaar which the seniors planned for next Sunday. It would be a comfort to try to help the earthquake victims in some small way.

'It will take my mind off things, Elizabeth,' Joan had said, an expression of quiet fortitude on her face.

It upset Elizabeth that she was not to be a monitor, after all. But it upset her even more that Joan had been stripped of the post.

'Kerry Dane's been too clever for us so far, Joan, but we're not going to let her win!' Elizabeth muttered darkly. 'We'll find some way – *some* way – of showing her up for what she is!'

By Sunday afternoon, Elizabeth was hitting the table-tennis ball with great venom and accuracy. It was an excellent way to relieve her feelings.

'Phew!' said Harry, as Elizabeth won their game with a beautiful smash.

'Your return just sat up and begged for a forehand smash, Harry!' laughed Elizabeth. 'You should try to spin it and keep it low, that's what Emma says. You ought to come to the coaching sessions, they're fun!'

'I'm not good enough,' said Harry. 'But you're getting brilliant. I'm sure you'll get into the team, Elizabeth.'

Most of her classmates were being very nice to her this weekend. She had worked so hard to get Emma elected. They felt sorry that she'd lost control of her temper and with it her chance of being monitor. It was sad about Joan, too. Belinda and Daniel, the new monitors, felt especially unhappy.

At that moment one of the seniors appeared.

'Ah, found you, Elizabeth,' Philippa smiled. 'A treat for you! A telephone call from your mother. Would you like to run and take it?'

Philippa felt sorry for the Naughtiest Girl too and the trouble that her emotions had got her into the previous day. It was nice that her mother had rung!

I wonder what Mummy wants? Elizabeth thought, as she hurried along to the little room called the Telephone Room. It was just a tiny box room with a comfortable chair and a low table. On the table was a coin-in-the-slot payphone.

Boys and girls from the second form upwards were allowed to receive calls from their family on a Sunday, and even to make outgoing calls if they were important. It was an exciting privilege. But Elizabeth had not expected to receive a telephone call so soon! The receiver lay on the table, waiting to be picked up.

'Hello, Mummy!'

'Hello, Elizabeth dear.'

Mrs Allen had rung about the flowers.

'Thank you! It was such a lovely surprise when Daddy brought them home. They're still as fresh as ever, even now. I've arranged them in the big vase on the hall table. I wish you could see them!'

'I can just imagine them, Mummy,' said Elizabeth, closing her eyes and doing so. Mrs

Allen loved flowers so and made wonderful arrangements. 'I'm glad you're pleased with them.'

'It must have been very interesting for you to meet Kerry Dane like that!' her mother was saying. 'I was so surprised that she didn't want to keep the flowers herself—'

'I think she had too much to carry, Mummy,' Elizabeth said hastily. The Naughtiest Girl had not, of course, told her father that the bouquet had been rescued from a dustbin. There'd hardly been time to explain all that! It was simpler just to say that the actress hadn't needed them. 'I expect she gets lots of flowers,' she added.

'It was still extremely kind of her to make us a gift of them,' continued Mrs Allen. 'I thought you would like to know how pleased I am. And, of course, I hope to find an address to write to. I would like to drop a thank you note to Miss Dane. I expect she has an agent in London . . .'

'Oh, Mummy, I shouldn't bother to do that!

I'm sure she would just find it embarrassing. Please don't bother to write a note!'

But her mother had become distracted.

'Oh, there's the doorbell!' said Mrs Allen. 'I have some friends coming to tea. They will be very impressed when they hear about the flowers. Thank you again, Elizabeth. How lovely to speak to you on the telephone.'

Elizabeth replaced the receiver and left the Telephone Room. It was a nice surprise to get a telephone call from her mother. But how she would hate it if Mrs Allen found out the agent's address and sent him a note for Kerry Dane!

If only she knew where she was! One day, when this was all over, she would tell her mother the whole story.

'Where's my table-tennis bat?' she asked John McTavish when she returned. He was having a knockabout with Daniel, now that the table had come free.

'I expect you took it with you to the Telephone Room, Elizabeth!' laughed John. 'We haven't got it!'

'Yes, so I did! And I've left it there, too. How silly of me!'

Elizabeth retraced her footsteps. She would pick up her bat and then go to have a shower before tea.

The door of the Telephone Room was ajar. Somebody else was already in there, she could hear them speaking. The telephone was in use again!

Elizabeth hovered outside the door, wondering if the person would mind her just creeping in to get the bat. Then, as she recognised the voice, she stiffened.

It was Kerry Dane.

She was gloating. Elizabeth could hear every word.

'Mummy, it was brilliant of you and Daddy to find Whyteleafe School for me. I didn't believe you when you said you'd found a school like this where the pupils are in charge! No stupid teachers will ever boss me around again . . .'

Then, a few moment's silence. Followed by laughter.

'Yes, of course it was cheeky of them at Horton High! Trying to behave as if I was still an ordinary schoolgirl. Trying to act as if I wasn't famous. It's different at this place. You said it would be. We can do what we like. And you'll never guess. I've been made head-girl! Instead of being bossed around by grown-ups, I'm in charge of the other pupils, with a boy called Thomas. It's going to be such fun, telling everybody what to do! There are one or two silly little rules, that's all. I'll tell you why I've rung, Mummy. Can you get some cash to me . . .'

More silence. And then, the voice became sulky:

'Oh, don't be silly, Mummy. I can't be bothered to explain about the other cash. Why's it difficult? Can't you send banknotes by registered post?' Kerry was becoming increasingly petulant. 'I need to be able to buy myself treats when I want to, Mummy!'

Elizabeth tiptoed away. She had heard enough! Her table-tennis bat could wait!

She raced off to find Joan and Julian.

Breathlessly, she told them everything she'd overheard.

'So *that's* why she's come to Whyteleafe School!' whistled Julian.

'Yes, she thinks there's no discipline here. That this is a soft school where she can do exactly what she likes!' said Elizabeth, outraged. 'But that's not how things work at Whyteleafe. A person like that can't be allowed to be head-girl! It's an insult! Surely we can do something—'

'There's nothing we *can* do, Elizabeth,' said Joan calmly, 'except be very, very patient. It can only be a matter of time now before her true nature reveals itself.'

'I'm not sure I can just sit around and wait for "time"!' exclaimed Elizabeth furiously.

Julian ruffled her hair and grinned.

'Always the bold, bad Elizabeth!' he observed. 'I'm afraid we haven't any choice, whether we like it or not.'

* * *

There was strawberry ice cream for tea that day but Elizabeth hardly tasted it as she spooned it down, silent and inwardly smouldering.

Looking across from the seniors' table, Emma saw how unhappy she seemed.

The senior girl came and sought her out later.

Emma was still very unhappy herself but she was determined not to let it show.

'Cheer up, Elizabeth!' she said lightly. 'I know how disappointed you must be feeling about the election result. But we must put a brave face on things, you know!' She smiled. 'We can't have people thinking we are bad losers, can we?'

'It's nothing to do with being a bad loser!' Elizabeth blurted out. 'It's just that Kerry Dane doesn't go with Whyteleafe School and she's certainly not a worthy person to be its head-girl!'

'Sssh, Elizabeth!' said Emma, unhappily. 'You really mustn't go around saying things like that. I forbid it. The election is behind us now and we have the result. Kerry is our new head-girl and I want you to tell me that you accept it.'

'I don't accept it, Emma,' replied Elizabeth, firmly. 'I'll *never* accept it. I can't even bring myself to go to the next School Meeting. Not if she's still head-girl!'

Emma's eyes widened.

'Stop it, Elizabeth! Of course Kerry will still be head-girl at the next Meeting! And of *course* you must go! If you miss another Meeting over this you will show a complete lack of self-discipline. You will be setting a bad example to the younger pupils in the school.'

Elizabeth tried to turn her eyes away.

'Look at me, Elizabeth,' said Emma, gently. Elizabeth met her gaze. 'I want you to make me a promise. Even if privately you can't accept Kerry as head-girl, you are to *promise* not to miss another Meeting. Do you give me your promise?'

Elizabeth could see that she was making Emma unhappy. She swallowed.

'All right,' she mumbled. 'I promise.'

That night she took out her autograph book and gazed at its spoiled white leather cover, with tears in her eyes. Then she opened it. She found the words that Rita had written at the end of last term, a beautiful line of poetry.

Kerry Dane isn't good enough to step into Rita's shoes, thought Elizabeth. *She never was and she never will be. Only Emma will do! It's an outrage!*

But if the three friends tried to explain that to people, they'd only think, as Emma had gently tried to point out, that it was a case of Elizabeth and Co being bad losers.

Julian and Joan were right. They would have to bide their time.

I only hope my patience can last out, thought Elizabeth, restlessly, as she tossed and turned and tried to get to sleep. *I only hope nothing unexpected takes place, to push me over the edge.*

But that was exactly what happened.

* * *

It was after school, the following Friday.

It had turned out to be a very good week for Elizabeth, in other respects. She was enjoying her new lessons in the second form. And, although it was horrid not being a monitor after all, Belinda and Daniel were both very kind about it. They kept saying that they weren't really cut out to be monitors and Elizabeth and Joan would have been so much better. She was also pleased that Miss Ranger had made her top in English this week.

But the best thing of all about the week was that she had got into the table-tennis squad! After the second coaching session, Mr Warlow's list had gone up on the noticeboard – and there was her name! Patrick was only first reserve, in spite of his excellent new bat.

Tomorrow, Saturday, they'd travel by minibus to St Faith's and play their first match. How exciting that was going to be!

Before that, however, Elizabeth was trying to steel herself for the weekly Meeting. It was taking place on Friday this week. That morning, a dark cloud had descended over her head. When lessons were over, she went for a walk around the school grounds, trying to calm herself.

'I just dread going into the hall today!' she muttered to herself. 'Even though I promised Emma I would. It will be too unbearable to sit there in silence and watch Kerry Dane being a drama queen. Acting the part of being a fine head-girl! Everybody looking up to her! I really cannot bear it . . .'

Suddenly Elizabeth stopped. She had heard a funny little sound. She looked all around.

There it was again! It seemed to be coming from the shrubbery.

It was the sound of someone sobbing.

10 Elizabeth is defiant

'What's wrong, Rupert?' asked Elizabeth, diving in amongst the bushes. 'Why are you hiding? Has somebody been bullying you?'

The small new boy gazed up at Elizabeth, his cheeks stained with tears. He had hidden so that nobody would think that he was a cry-baby. Slowly he brought his sobs under control. Elizabeth gently dried his eyes with her clean white handkerchief.

'Well, have they?'

Rupert shook his head.

'Then why have you been crying?' coaxed Elizabeth. 'What's the matter?'

'Mustn't talk about it,' he muttered. 'Mustn't let people know I'm greedy.'

His lip trembled and he started sobbing again.

'I'm not greedy!' he wailed. 'I was going to share them with all my friends!'

'Share *what*, Rupert?' asked Elizabeth. 'You are allowed to tell me about it. And it will make you feel better. Share *what* exactly?'

The words came tumbling out.

'My chocolate soldiers grandfather sent me for my birthday! I was going to share them out at teatime. But she wouldn't listen to me. She took them away from me! She took them away!'

'Who did, Rupert?'

'Kerry did!'

Elizabeth stared at him in disbelief.

'The head-girl?'

Rupert nodded solemnly.

'When?'

'This afternoon. She needs them for the earthquake.'

The earthquake? Elizabeth frowned. Of course. The Earthquake Bazaar, next weekend. Kerry Dane was in charge of the sweet stall. But what a mean, horrid way to behave! She had no right to force the little boy to give up his birthday present for it!

Rupert looked scared and put a hand to his mouth.

'I promised not to tell anybody. Or else she'll tell everybody in the whole school I'm a very greedy little boy!'

Elizabeth bent down and gently placed an arm round his shoulders.

'You're not greedy, Rupert. Now listen to me. You're to go and wash your face and hands. It will soon be time for the Meeting. You're to stop worrying about this. It's just a – a horrid little mistake. Remember how I found your teddy bear for you, on the bus? Well – I'll make sure you get your chocolate soldiers back, too! Off you go!'

The fair-haired boy looked pleased and grateful.

'Oh, thank you!'

Elizabeth stood and watched him walk back to the school buildings. He turned and waved. Calmly she waved back but her cheeks were flushed with anger. What a despicable way for a head-girl to behave. What an abuse of power!

The real Kerry Dane, Elizabeth thought. *The mask has started to crack at last!*

She reached a decision. She had promised Emma to attend the Meeting.

Well, she would keep her promise!

And I know exactly what I'll do when I get there, thought Elizabeth, with a cheerful gleam in her eye.

'Silence!' shouted Thomas, banging the gavel loudly. 'I am trying to start the Meeting!'

The head-boy was angry. The children were refusing to settle down. They all kept chattering and turning round to look at Elizabeth Allen.

It was such an amazing sight.

The Naughtiest Girl was seated on the second form benches but she was facing the wrong way! She was sitting with her back to the platform.

What does Elizabeth think she's doing? wondered Emma, in dismay.

Elizabeth sat stiffly on her bench. Instead of facing the head-boy and girl and the monitors, she had turned her back on them and sat facing the other way. Her arms were folded stubbornly, in silent protest.

'Quiet everybody!' cried Thomas.

The children forced themselves to stop looking at Elizabeth. The chatter died to a whisper and then to complete silence.

'Thank you,' said Thomas. 'We have a lot of business to get through today. But before we begin, would Elizabeth please be kind enough to stand up and face the right way. I wish to speak to her.'

Elizabeth did so.

'What is the meaning of this tomfoolery, Elizabeth?' he asked.

'I do not wish to face the platform,' announced Elizabeth, in clear ringing tones. 'I do not accept Kerry Dane as head-girl. She has proved herself an unfit person and I think she should resign.'

The school listened in astonishment. Julian

and Joan exchanged troubled glances. What had provoked this? They had all agreed they would have to be patient. Did Elizabeth know what she was doing? Was she not being very hot-headed?

Next to Thomas on the platform, Kerry Dane cast her eyes down. Her heart was bumping with anger. Who was this dreadful girl they called the Naughtiest Girl? What was this all about?

'I see,' replied Thomas, calmly. 'That is a very dramatic statement, Elizabeth. Perhaps you would be good enough to explain to the Meeting your reasons for making it.'

'I will be very pleased to, Thomas.'

Elizabeth pointed accusingly at Kerry Dane.

'Kerry thinks that this is a school where she can do whatever she likes. She has behaved today no better than a common bully. Little Rupert was sent some chocolate soldiers for his birthday, by his grandfather. This afternoon Kerry Dane forced him to hand them over to her for her stall at the Earthquake Bazaar.'

A shocked gasp ran round the hall.

Kerry Dane leapt to her feet at once, a pained expression on her face.

'Elizabeth, how could you say such a thing?' she asked sorrowfully. 'How could you even *think* such a thing? I am very, very hurt.'

She then looked down at the juniors, sitting cross-legged on the floor at the front of the hall. Her eyes lighted on the smallest one, with very fair hair.

'Stand up please, Rupert,' she said, in a kindly voice. 'I think we need to sort this out together, don't you?'

The small boy rose.

But he was left standing there, nervously blinking, as the young actress came to the edge of the platform and looked straight past him. With arms out-flung, she began to address the school, a radiant expression on her face, her lips sweetly smiling.

'First of all, this is exactly the right moment to say thank you! Thank you all for the wonderful response you've made so far! All the lovely things you've been bringing me for the sweet stall. Every day you come and see me and bring your goodies, knowing the money raised will help the earthquake victims. I find your generosity very touching. And I found Rupert's gift today perhaps the most touching of all . . .'

She then looked down and fixed her eyes on the small boy, who was now beginning to feel frightened and overwhelmed.

'Look at me, please, Rupert.'

The small child gazed up at the figure towering over him.

'Now, Rupert, where did Elizabeth get this funny idea from? Have you been making up naughty stories? Did you regret it afterwards, giving your chocolate soldiers away? Was it something you did on the spur of the moment because you felt sorry for the earthquake victims? But you were so insistent at the time, Rupert! Don't you remember? You told me you thought it would be a very greedy thing to keep them. Didn't you?'

Rupert gazed up into those mesmerising brown eyes. He was blinking non-stop, overcome with confusion. He was like a frightened rabbit in the thrall of a stoat.

'Now, think hard, Rupert. Don't you remember?' repeated Kerry.

She was daring him to contradict her. His sense of confusion increased.

'I – I can't remember exactly. I s'pose I must have done. I don't know. Elizabeth asked me why I was crying and I s'pose . . .'

Arabella whispered to Patrick behind her hand.

'Elizabeth making up naughty stories, more like it!'

Kerry was finishing Rupert's sentence for him.

'You knew you'd given me your soldiers but then you wished you hadn't and it made you cry. But you didn't dare tell Elizabeth how silly you'd been, so you made up a naughty little story instead! Now, please don't start crying again! There's no need to get upset about it. We all make mistakes.'

'You may sit down now, Rupert,' intervened Thomas, feeling sorry for the child. 'And don't be a cry-baby. Nobody's going to punish you. Think carefully in future before you give things away. Make quite sure that you really want to do so. Only babies give things to people and then want to have them back! You're a big boy now, remember.'

'Yes, Thomas.'

The child hastily sat down, feeling tearful and totally confused.

Elizabeth had listened to the whole exchange in stunned silence.

What a brilliant actress Kerry Dane was. What an Oscar-winning performance!

Thomas now spoke to the Naughtiest Girl, while the whole school listened with avid interest. Julian and Joan were feeling only total dismay.

'We already know, Elizabeth, that you have found it very difficult to accept the results of last week's election. And that you have lost your chance to be a monitor because of it. But

you must know that the way you just spoke to
our new head-girl is not something that can be
tolerated. She has been properly elected and
she must be shown respect. You will please
make a public apology to Kerry.'

'I certainly shall not,' said Elizabeth defiantly.

Thomas bit his lip. He felt worried and upset
but he dared not show it.

'Then you must leave the Meeting at once.'

Elizabeth barely heard him. She was already
striding out of the hall. Her eyes were misted
with anger and there was only one thought on
her mind.

11   The naughtiest girl wins through

I don't believe Kerry Dane for one instant! she thought. *I'm going to get Rupert's chocolates back for him!*

Elizabeth raced upstairs to the seniors' common room. She knew that she was strictly forbidden to enter without permission, but she didn't care. There was nobody to stop her. The entire school was seated safely at the Meeting.

I know where they keep everything for the Bazaar! thought Elizabeth. *It's going to be quite easy to get Rupert's soldiers! I promised him!*

Elizabeth was quite positive that Rupert had been telling her the truth. It was Kerry Dane who'd been telling the naughty little stories, as she called them! But how could the school know how awful she was? That she had actually taken a junior's birthday present away from him? Even for a good cause, it was such an unbelievable thing to do!

But that, Elizabeth felt quite sure, was exactly what had happened.

Goodness only knows why, thought Elizabeth, as she slipped into the big common room and headed for the cupboard in the corner. *But I'll see that Rupert gets his birthday present back if it's the last thing I ever do at Whyteleafe!*

At her boldest and most reckless, Elizabeth found the key to the cupboard. She knew where it was because she'd been here with Daniel when he'd handed in some pottery for Philippa's craft stall. She turned the key in the lock.

The cupboard door creaked open.

The shelves were neatly labelled: Craft Stall . . . White Elephant . . . Sweet Stall . . .

The shelf set aside for the sweet stall was already nearly full. There were sweets of every description, some of them shop sweets, many of them home-made. There were jars of home-made peppermints, toffees and coconut ice.

There were at least three sugar mice. There was Arabella's fudge, too. Elizabeth recognised the box. How busy all the children had been, eager to please the young film star.

She frowned, beginning to feel uneasy.

'It's true what she said, then. The children *have* been giving her stacks of things for the sweet stall. The shelf's almost full and there's still a whole week to go before the Bazaar! So there's hardly any danger of her stall not being a success, then . . .'

It made her mean behaviour seem more unbelievable than ever.

'I know!' Elizabeth said to herself. 'Perhaps there isn't very much chocolate. Everybody's giving her sweets but she wants to have some chocolate things to go with them.'

Elizabeth then checked each item on the shelf, very carefully.

And then she realised something.

It wasn't that there was not *very much* chocolate.

There was no chocolate at all!

'Even Rupert's chocolate soldiers aren't here,' she realised, in surprise. She relocked the cupboard and carefully replaced the key in its hiding place, puzzled. 'What *can* she have done with them?'

Elizabeth came out of the seniors' common room and closed the door. She looked up and down the corridor.

'It must be that she simply hasn't bothered to put them in the cupboard yet,' Elizabeth decided. 'Yes, that will be it! They must still be somewhere in her room.'

Slowly, hesitantly, she walked along the corridor until she came to a door. It said: HEAD-GIRL, PRIVATE. She hesitated for many seconds. Much as she hated Kerry Dane, it seemed a very wrong thing to do.

But then she thought of Rupert, and his tears, and the terrible injustice he had suffered.

She turned the handle and eased open the door of Kerry Dane's private quarters.

The Meeting was in full swing. On the

platform, the head-boy and girl had just been in a huddle with the monitors and come to a decision. Kerry and Thomas returned to their special table. It was Kerry's turn to pick up the gavel and bang for silence.

'Quiet, please, everybody!' she smiled. What a satisfying sound that gavel made. How quickly it brought the Meeting to order! She was beginning to enjoy herself again. 'The Meeting has now decided on the matter of punishment for the three pupils who walked out of last week's Meeting,' she announced. 'We have listened to the representations made by Belinda and Daniel on behalf of the two girls. And the Meeting has agreed that the losing of the monitorships is sufficient punishment for their last week's behaviour. As far as Elizabeth's behaviour today is concerned, the Meeting has decided that she is not a fit person to represent the school at table-tennis.'

Kerry had to fight hard to conceal her glee. This was all such fun!

Julian and Joan looked at one another in

dismay. They had been sitting there, discussing
Elizabeth's latest walkout in growing alarm.
They had hoped all week that Elizabeth would
not lose patience and do something reckless.
But she had! She had tried to catch Kerry Dane
out on quite the wrong thing! The story that
Rupert had told Elizabeth was really rather
preposterous. And, even if there had been a
grain of truth in it, Kerry Dane had been much
too clever to be caught out!

'Poor Elizabeth,' whispered Joan. 'We
warned her to be patient.'

'The Naughtiest Girl doesn't know the
meaning of the word,' Julian whispered back.
'Something like this was bound to happen.'

'Now we come to the matter of the boy,' the
head-girl continued. 'Would you stand up,
please, er—'

Julian got lazily to his feet, a mocking
expression in his eyes.

'My name's Julian,' he said. 'Julian Holland.'

'Yes, well – er – Julian. The Meeting has
decided that you must apologise in front

of the whole school and—'

'No!' shouted a voice from the back.

Elizabeth came running into the hall, panting for breath. She was holding something aloft. She halted and everyone turned round to look at her.

'You're the one who must apologise in front of the whole school, Kerry Dane,' she cried out. 'You must apologise to Rupert for your despicable behaviour. For stealing his chocolates and pretending you wanted them for the Bazaar. When all the time—'

Slowly, deliberately, Elizabeth began to walk towards the platform. There was a high colour in her cheeks and a scornful expression on her face. She was holding aloft a floral patterned wastepaper basket. It had come from Kerry Dane's room.

' – you wanted to eat them yourself.'

The head-girl turned white as she recognised the wastepaper basket.

What happened next was very un-head-girl-like.

With a cry of fury, she leapt down from the platform and raced towards Elizabeth, her golden mane flying out behind her. Her face was contorted with rage.

'How dare you go into my private room!' she screamed. 'How dare you go poking around in my waste-paper basket—!'

She took a wild swing at Elizabeth. It knocked the wastepaper basket out of her hands and sent it flying to the ground.

Glittering tinfoil wrappings scattered in all directions. There were loud gasps throughout the hall.

Julian nipped across and picked one up. Quickly he straightened it out. A soldier's face appeared and then the body, dressed in bright red tinfoil uniform. Silently, Julian held it up and displayed it to the shocked, silent children all around him. At the back of the hall, Miss Belle and Miss Best and Mr Johns had gone very pale.

'The wrapping from a chocolate soldier, I presume,' he said drily.

'It's mine!' cried Rupert, his little voice piping up from the front of the hall. 'It's all eaten! I didn't give them to her. I didn't, I didn't. She took all my soldiers!'

'And this stupid school has taken all my money!' blazed Kerry Dane. 'I need to be able to buy chocolate when I crave some, don't I? As soon as some more money comes through, I'll replace your silly little soldiers. They weren't even all that chocolatey!'

Gradually she began to regain her composure. The whole school watched, open-mouthed, as she turned on her heel. Slowly, majestically, she walked back to the platform. Her chin was thrust forward, her head held high.

'I would like to remind you all of something. I *am* the head-girl of this school, you know.'

She remounted the platform and took her place beside Thomas. She did not even notice the horrified expression on the head-boy's face, or on the faces of the monitors behind him.

'Now, to more important matters,' she

began. 'The question of Julian Holland—'

Suddenly a strange sound filled the hall. It was a sound that had never before been heard at a School Meeting. It was started by some of the fourth formers.

It was the sound of booing.

Within moments the whole school joined in the booing and hissing, drowning out the sound of Kerry Dane's voice.

'Resign!' cried the children.

'Resign! Resign!'

Elizabeth, Joan and Julian exchanged joyful looks.

'We want Emma!' cried the Naughtiest Girl. 'Emma for head-girl!'

The booing stopped. Everybody clapped and cheered and stamped their feet, taking up Elizabeth's cry.

'We want Emma!'

'We want Emma!'

Kerry Dane gazed at the sea of faces in disbelief. She had suffered the disapproval of many teachers at her last school and it had annoyed her. But this was something very much worse. The disapproval of other pupils, of her school mates, was really horrid. It was humiliating.

She sank down in her chair, deeply shocked.

Thomas picked up the gavel and brought the Meeting to order. He knew that even William and Rita would, at a moment like this, have needed help from the joint headmistresses and the senior master. He looked to the back of the hall.

'Please, can you give the Meeting your advice?' he asked them. 'What should we do?'

Miss Best rose to her feet.

'The Meeting must follow its own advice, Thomas. It could hardly be clearer! Might we suggest that you now declare the Meeting closed? Next week, when Kerry has resigned and been replaced by her runner-up in the election, the slate can be wiped clean and a fresh start made.'

'Thank you, Miss Best,' replied Thomas, looking pleased.

He smiled across at Emma and his smile was returned.

Shortly after, Kerry Dane came down from the platform for the last time. She knew that she had no hope of ever returning to it.

12   *A lovely Meeting*

It had been a chastening experience for the young film star. But the days that followed were worse. The seniors tried to be friendly towards her but they found it very hard after what had taken place. Even kindly Emma found it difficult, although she tried her best.

The rest of the school, with few exceptions, shunned her.

To the many children who had seen *Zara's Journey* in the school holidays and admired her as Zara, the shock of discovering her true nature had been very severe; just as it had been, that day in London, for Elizabeth and Joan. Kerry was left to her own devices a great deal. She had plenty of time on her hands to think and to contemplate. She was not used to this. She began to feel unhappy and to think about her real self and whether she liked what she found.

In the days before the next School Meeting, Elizabeth by contrast was in very sunny spirits. She was allowed to play in the table-tennis match after all, and did well. Belinda and Daniel insisted on standing down as second form monitors. Mr Leslie agreed that Joan and Elizabeth should take their places and be monitors after all.

Thomas, with Emma as the new head-girl, called in all the monitors early in the week, to decide how much money the children should be allowed at the next Meeting. They would need a lot more than usual, for the Earthquake Bazaar.

Elizabeth was proud to have her opinion asked and to be part of the running of the school. She knew that she was going to enjoy every moment as a second form monitor with her best friend Joan.

But she was beginning to notice how much time Kerry Dane spent on her own. For the very first time she began to feel slightly sorry for her.

One day, after school, when Elizabeth and Julian came back from a pony ride, they found her on her own as usual, by the stables. She was stroking one of the ponies.

'Hello, Kerry.'

The three of them stood and talked for a while. Elizabeth was as forthright as ever. She knew no other way.

'I was shunned when I first came to Whyteleafe, Kerry, so I know just what you're going through!' she said cheerfully. 'I was very spoilt, like you, and I made it my business to be as horrid as I could.'

'Did you?' asked Kerry in surprise.

'She wanted to be sent home, that's why,' explained Julian, glancing at Elizabeth in amusement. He never knew what his friend was going to say next. He always had to expect the unexpected. 'That's how she got her nickname, the Naughtiest Girl in the School. She didn't want to be at boarding school! She's not really horrid, by the way.'

'You mean, she isn't like me?' commented Kerry, drily.

'No, I wasn't anything like you!' Elizabeth declared truthfully. 'But I *did* behave badly. And I definitely remember that nobody liked me.'

'So what happened then?' asked Kerry.

'Oh, it doesn't last,' replied Elizabeth, airily. 'Not if you mend your ways.'

Kerry patted the horse once more and then walked slowly back to school.

'I don't think she's a person who can *ever* mend her ways,' smiled Julian, as they rubbed down the ponies. 'She's too far gone for that.'

'Perhaps she'll make a tiny little start some time,' said Elizabeth hopefully. 'You never know.'

And at the Meeting the next day, that was exactly what Kerry did.

She sat, pale and silent, on the senior benches while Thomas and Emma moved smoothly through Complaints and Grumbles. When, finally, they reached Any Other Business, she raised her hand.

'Yes, Kerry?' asked Emma, encouragingly.

Kerry rose. She was trembling slightly. She was suffering from stage fright, something she'd never experienced before. But she was determined to go through with this. She held aloft a large box of chocolate soldiers. She had borrowed two weeks' allowance in advance, to be able to buy them. It had been hard work finding them, too.

Her words came out in a rush.

'I'd like to present Rupert with this box of chocolate soldiers. And I'd like to apologise to him in front of the whole school for what I did.'

At a nod from the platform, the little boy came running over and took the box. His face was shining.

'I'm sorry they're not exactly the same as the other ones, Rupert,' said Kerry.

'They're bigger! They're better!' Rupert beamed, his faith in Whyteleafe School restored. 'I will share them, I promise!'

There were approving murmurs around the hall. Some people clapped. From her monitor's chair up on the platform, Elizabeth saw the look on Julian's face and laughed. It was satisfying to think he could sometimes be wrong.

It had turned out to be a lovely Meeting.

Soon after that, Kerry Dane had a birthday. It was no longer a legal requirement for her to remain at school. She had received a batch of letters from her agent in London and amongst them was another film offer. In consultation with her parents, it was decided that she should forego her certificate exams and leave school. She could now become a full-time actress.

From the joint headmistresses' window, on the day she left Whyteleafe School, the Beauty and the Beast watched her walk towards her father's small blue car. Her hair was as golden as corn in the sunshine as she stood waiting for her luggage to be loaded aboard.

'All that glisters is not gold,' sighed Miss Best, looking at that halo.

'She certainly glistered though, didn't she?' observed Miss Belle. 'If, alas, not gold.'

'She was not with us very long,' continued Miss Best, 'but I would like to feel that she leaves Whyteleafe a better person than when she came.'

'Elizabeth Allen saw to that!' smiled Miss Belle. 'I will never understand how it was that Elizabeth and her friends divined her true nature long before the rest of us.'

'Nor me,' agreed Miss Best.

But it was no mystery to Kerry Dane. Not any longer.

Amongst the batch of letters that her agent had forwarded from his London office, had been a very odd little note:

Dear Miss Dane
Thank you so much for the beautiful
flowers you gave to my daughter Elizabeth
last week. She was about to catch her train

*to boarding school and so passed them to
her father to bring safely home. They are
very much appreciated and still as fresh as
ever.*

Yours sincerely

Audrey Allen

Slowly, the truth had dawned.

Cringing in embarrassment at the memory
of their encounter, Kerry had gone to find
Elizabeth and to apologise. She was playing
chess with Julian.

'It's all right, Kerry,' Elizabeth had replied.
'But it just shows you should always be nice to
everybody you meet. Even old tramps and
beggars in the street. You never know where
you might meet them again.'

'Yes, I can see that,' had been Kerry's humble
reply. 'I suppose it's cruel and silly to be horrid
to someone for no good reason.'

Especially when it's the Naughtiest Girl,
thought Julian, with a smile.

ABOUT THE AUTHOR

Anne Digby was born in Kingston upon Thames and is married with one son and three daughters. As a child she loved reading and the first full length book she ever read on her own was the Blyton translation of Jean de Brunoff's *The Story of Babar, the little Elephant*, from the French. From there is was a short step to enjoying Enid Blyton's own adventure stories of which her favourite was *The Secret Mountain*. Anne has now had over thirty children's novels published of her own, including the *Trebizon* school series and the *Me, Jill Robinson* series of family adventures. This is her fifth book in the *Enid Blyton's Naughtiest Girl* series, the rest of which are listed below.

THE NAUGHTIEST GIRL KEEPS A SECRET
Elizabeth intends never to be naughty again. But then John entrusts her with his secret . . .

THE NAUGHTIEST GIRL HELPS A FRIEND
How *can* the naughtiest girl be good at camp with horrible Arabella in the very same tent?

THE NAUGHTIEST GIRL SAVES THE DAY
Elizabeth longs to star in the school summer play, but she will have to behave. Can she manage it?

WELL DONE, THE NAUGHTIEST GIRL
The worst girl in the school – or the best? It's the end of term and Elizabeth's fate will soon be decided!

ORDER FORM

Enid Blyton

0 340 72758 6	THE NAUGHTIEST GIRL IN THE SCHOOL	£3.50	❏
0 340 72759 4	THE NAUGHTIEST GIRL AGAIN	£3.50	❏
0 340 72760 8	THE NAUGHTIEST GIRL IS A MONITOR	£3.50	❏
0 340 72761 6	HERE'S THE NAUGHTIEST GIRL!	£3.50	❏

Anne Digby

0 340 72762 4	THE NAUGHTIEST GIRL KEEPS A SECRET	£3.50	❏
0 340 72763 2	THE NAUGHTIEST GIRL HELPS A FRIEND	£3.50	❏
0 340 74423 5	THE NAUGHTIEST GIRL SAVES THE DAY	£3.50	❏
0 340 74424 3	WELL DONE, THE NAUGHTIEST GIRL	£3.50	❏

All Hodder Children's books are available at your local bookshop, or can be ordered direct from the publisher. Just tick the titles you would like and complete the details below. Prices and availability are subject to change without prior notice.

Please enclose a cheque or postal order made payable to *Bookpoint Ltd*, and send to: Hodder Children's Books, 39 Milton Park, Abingdon, OXON OX14 4TD, UK.
Email Address: orders@bookpoint.co.uk

If you would prefer to pay by credit card, our call centre team would be delighted to take your order by telephone. Our direct line *01235 400414* (lines open 9.00 am–6.00 pm Monday to Saturday, 24 hour message answering service). Alternatively you can send a fax on *01235 400454*.

TITLE		FIRST NAME		SURNAME	

ADDRESS	
DAYTIME TEL:		POST CODE	

If you would prefer to pay by credit card, please complete:
Please debit my Visa/Access/Diner's Card/American Express (delete as applicable) card no:

Signature .... Expiry Date ....
If you would NOT like to receive further information on our products please tick the box. ❏